The She-Devil
in the Mirror

THE SHE-DEVIL
IN THE MIRROR

HORACIO CASTELLANOS MOYA

———

TRANSLATED BY KATHERINE SILVER

ALMA BOOKS

ALMA BOOKS LTD
London House
243–253 Lower Mortlake Road
Richmond
Surrey TW9 2LL
United Kingdom
www.almabooks.com

First published in UK by Alma Books Limited in 2010
First published in Spanish by Tusquets Editores in 2000
This translation first published by New Directions in 2009
Copyright © 2000 by Ediciones Linteo S.L.
Copyright © 2000 by Horacio Castellano Moya
Translation copyright © 2009 by Katherine Silver

Horacio Castellano Moya and Katherine Silver assert their moral right to be
identified as the author and translator of this work in accordance with the Copyright,
Designs and Patents Act 1988

This is a work of fiction. Names, characters, places and incidents either are the
product of the author's imagination or are used fictitiously, and any resemblance to
actual persons, living or dead, business establishments, events or locales is entirely
coincidental.

Printed in Great Britain by CPI Cox & Wyman, Reading, Berkshire

ISBN: 978-1-84688-104-6

The She-Devil
in the Mirror

CONTENTS

CONTENTS

To Tania Mata Parducci, Otoniel Martínez
and Patricia Ardón, Lucrecia Ardón, Ana Tomico

1. The Wake

How could such a tragedy have happened, my dear. I just spent the whole morning with Olga María at her boutique in the Villas Españolas Mall, I went with her to check on a special order. It's unbelievable. I still can't believe it; it's like a nightmare. I don't know why they're taking so long to get her ready: it's already five thirty, and they still haven't brought her out. It's that magistrate, he took his sweet time. He's a disgrace. The poor thing, stretched out there on her living-room floor, everybody and his brother coming and going through the house. How horrible. They let me know right away: Sergio, Olga María's brother, called my house and said something terrible had happened, Olga María had been "mortally wounded" during an attempted robbery. That's what he said: "mortally wounded". I couldn't believe it – I'd been with her just an hour and a half earlier. We left the boutique and walked to the parking lot together. She said she was going to pick the girls up at school and then she'd call me in the afternoon. No wonder Sergio's call caught me totally by surprise. I asked him which hospital they'd taken her to. He said she wasn't in a hospital, she was lying dead on her living-room floor, and Marito had taken the girls to Doña Olga's. I was in shock. I couldn't even react. Then I said, "I'm on my way." I drove like a madwoman, like I was on drugs, my dear, I don't know how I managed to avoid an

3

accident. So many images of her raced through my mind, and the last words we'd exchanged that morning, about how happy she was that sales at the boutique were up and about how she was trying to patch up her relationship with Marito. And then something like this – it's so unfair. Anyway, their house is in Colonia La Sultana, and I live in Santa Tecla, so it took me only ten minutes to get there. The police were already there. I dashed out of my car, I wanted to prove to myself that it wasn't true, Olga María was still alive, and everything had been a terrible mistake. But there was her body, stretched out on the living-room rug next to the sofa in a pool of blood, covered with a white sheet. I knelt down and lifted the edge of the sheet: the hole in her head was small, but all her brains had poured out the back. Oh, my dear, I felt horrible – I even felt like vomiting. But I was too upset to even cry. I covered her back up. Sergio placed his hands on my shoulders and told me he needed me to be with the girls, they'd killed her in cold blood right in front of them, they were still in shock when Marito came to get them. Imagine that: those murderers killed Olga María right in front of the girls. It's unforgivable. They're taking their sweet time, they should bring her out any minute, a lot of people are starting to arrive. We chose a black-satin dress for her, very elegant. I want to see how it looks. Doña Olga had her doubts, but finally she followed my advice: it is her prettiest dress, it'll look best on her. Sergio insisted I go to their mother's to help her with the girls, because Marito had to get back to the house to deal with all the legalities, after all he is her

4

husband, the owner of the house, he's the one who's responsible for everything. Poor Marito, he's devastated. I didn't see him till later. We must have crossed paths, him on his way back to the house and me on my way to Doña Olga's. I was so eager to give the girls a hug, protect them, somehow make them forget what they'd seen. But halfway there, I broke down, it was horrible, my dear, I was choking and I couldn't breathe; I managed to pull off the road, then I started crying uncontrollably – my forehead on the steering wheel, I was crying for Olga María, for the girls, for Marito, for myself, because if I didn't get it off my chest it would only get worse later. When I got there, a doctor was talking to the girls. Doña Olga seemed composed, strong, she wasn't even crying, though you could see in her body how tortured she was. She told me they'd just given the girls a sedative, they were very upset, the best thing for them now was to get some rest instead of going over and over what they'd seen, that's what the doctor recommended. I hugged them, trying to control myself: I didn't want them to see me falling apart. Little Olga just turned ten, she's so grown up, so pretty, just like her mother, the same expressions, intelligent like her, too; Raquelita looks more like Marito, and she's a bit withdrawn, maybe because she's the youngest. They've always called me Auntie, even though we're not related, Olga María taught them to call me that: Auntie Laura. We were best friends, had been ever since we started at the American School – imagine that, twenty-three years ago. Finally, they're bringing her out. Come on, come with me, let's see how she looks. Look at those gorgeous flower arrangements: Marito's advertising agency sent them over. I told you that's her best dress – don't you think she looks gorgeous, they did a good job on her, you can barely even see the hole in her head. Life is a catastrophe. How could this have happened to her? You went to her last birthday party, remember? She was so happy to be turning thirty – she said the best part of life was just beginning, always so optimistic, so vivacious. Those sons of bitches, those cowards, they should all be killed. Doesn't her hair look great? It's just like she used to wear it for parties, Mercedes herself came from the beauty salon to do it. They're truly evil, all they wanted to do was kill her, they didn't steal anything, they didn't even try to. That's what little Olga told me this afternoon: he snuck up on them in the garage as they were getting out of the car, then forced them into the living room and there, without a word, he shot Olga María in the chest, then one to the head to finish her off. Disgraceful. Makes me so angry. More people are starting to arrive – let's go sit down. Look, here comes Marito. Sergio said he was going home to change clothes. Doña Olga and the girls will be here around seven, those poor dears, those girls have behaved so well, it's amazing how grown up they are. The one I'm worried about is Marito, he seems fragile, I don't know what he'd have done without Sergio. It's been a crazy afternoon. I spent about an hour at Doña Olga's, trying to distract the girls until the sedatives kicked in so they'd fall asleep. That's when little Olga told me about the murderer and how all he wanted was to kill Olga María: she told him to take the car, whatever he wanted, just don't hurt them, especially not the girls, but he didn't want anything, he just wanted to kill her, like someone had sent him, like he'd been given explicit instructions. Something smells rotten, because Olga María couldn't have any enemies. That's exactly what I told those insolent policemen who came to Doña Olga's asking for the girls; they wanted to question them, they said, because they were the only ones who saw the killer, they urgently needed a description of the murderer so they could make a composite sketch – they kept insisting it was very important. But the doctor said the girls shouldn't be disturbed – I told them – and anyway they were already asleep, so they'd better put off their questioning till tomorrow. But they were pig-headed, especially the boss, the one who said his name was Deputy Chief Handal, what a pig of a man – that's why we're in the mess we're in: the police spend their time harassing defenceless little girls instead of catching criminals. That's what I told him. No reaction. He just repeated that the sooner they got a description of the suspect the easier it would be to organize a manhunt and capture him. But I wasn't going to let those rude men wake up the girls. I stood my ground and told them they would have to wait a couple of hours until the girls woke up, and if the girls ended up with some permanent psychological damage, I would hold them responsible – Handal and that other nasty man who said his name was Detective Villalta – and that wouldn't be the end of it because I'd sue them, and

7

I'm not just some nobody, they couldn't mess with me, they'd better be very careful and show more respect or they'd soon find out who they were dealing with. But little Olga hadn't fallen asleep yet, she was lying down and dozing – a bit dazed from the sedatives – and what with the ruckus those policemen were making, she woke up. She got out of bed and appeared in the doorway and asked what was going on – maybe she'd got scared that the policemen were murderers, like the one who'd just killed Olga María. These two gentlemen, I explained to her, were policemen investigating her mother's death, and she should go back to bed because they were just about to leave. But this Deputy Chief Handal shoved his way in front of me and started interrogating little Olga – such a snake, they've got no respect for anybody, the pigs – and they took advantage of little Olga's innocence to get her to tell them what she'd already told me: that the murderer didn't want anything, all he wanted was to kill Olga María. The Deputy Chief asked little Olga to repeat every detail of the story three times, and he kept asking her questions – what a degenerate – then he called in some creep with a moustache, who was supposed to make a sketch based on the girl's information. Little Olga said the murderer was tall and heavy-set, a great big guy, clean-shaven, with very short hair, like a soldier's, and he was wearing blue jeans and white tennis shoes, like the kind astronauts wear, she said. The Deputy Chief asked her if she remembered any other details, anything out of the ordinary that would help them identify the suspect. Little

Olga said he walked like Robocop, that robot policeman on television. I warned the Deputy Chief to leave the girl alone, not to take advantage of her, who knows what damage it could do – she'd just taken a strong sedative. But that Handal creep kept at it: Was he alone? Did little Olga see the car he drove away in? Was she aware of anybody else in the street? Did the housekeeper show up before or after the crime had been committed? Oh no, not her, not our Julita, how could they possibly suspect her, I butted in, what a pig, Julita's practically raised Olga María, and now she's almost fifty, what are they thinking, she's worked for Doña Olga and Olga María her entire life, she's totally trustworthy, how could he be such an idiot. Doña Olga agreed. Little Olga explained that Julita came into the living room after the shots were fired, she was in the laundry room in the back of the house – she was the one who called Marito and Sergio and Doña Olga, and she was the one who ran to get help from the neighbours. You see those people coming in now: they work at Marito's agency – don't they look young? The tall one in the brown suit with curly hair and little round glasses, yes, the good-looking one, that's the new marketing director Marito just hired. Olga María told me about him, and she was right, he's very handsome. Anyway, as I was saying, once they finished with little Olga, this Deputy Chief Handal said he wanted to ask me a few questions, alone, seeing as how I'd known the victim so well, how I'd been her best friend, maybe I could help him, give him a few leads he could follow up on to find out what happened.

But I suspected he had something nasty up his sleeve, people like that – so crass, so degenerate, so dirty-minded – I've always known about policemen like him, that's why I was on my guard, I didn't want him to think he could catch me off guard. And it was just as I'd feared: the Deputy Chief asked me if I knew of any enemies Olga María or Marito might have, or maybe they had a big debt, or if there was an employee who'd threatened them after getting fired, or, with all due respect – those were his words, brazen man, "with all due respect" – if Olga María had had any extramarital relationships, maybe there was a disappointed lover, someone who might want to hurt her. That's when I got furious: he was a total idiot, I shouted at him, a complete boor, whatever made him think I was going to talk about my best friend's private life to some nobody like him, where could he possibly have got such an idea, how could he suspect such an honest, honourable woman, someone so devoted to her family and her work, what a scandalous insinuation; Olga María didn't have any enemies, nobody would ever dream of wanting to kill her, it had to have been a mistake or the act of a madman. I almost threw them out of the apartment, that's how dreadful they were, like mangy dogs. That's when Cuca, Sergio's wife, arrived: she was crying her head off, asking if the girls were all right, if Doña Olga needed anything. Here come Cheli and Conchita, Olga María's assistants at the boutique, you know them, don't you? They look so *comme il faut*, they adored Olga María, they've been working for her ever since she first opened the boutique, who knows what'll happen to them now. Marito will have to decide, or Doña Olga, whether to sell or not. As I was saying, Cuca arrived and we left her to look after the girls so Doña Olga and I could go to Olga María's house to make sure they fixed her up as best as possible. We took my car. Doña Olga had taken some strong sedatives – the poor woman is pretty old and unwell, and the doctor told her not to go to the scene of the crime, just the sight of it could do her great harm, she should wait till they took her to the funeral home. Sergio agreed and managed to convince her to wait. But when we got to Olga María's house, her body was still there. That's what I'm telling you: the magistrate is a stupid old drunk, he must have been out partying with his secretaries, I'm sure of it, that's why he took so long and why we couldn't prevent Doña Olga from seeing her daughter with her head blown to bits. But Marito and I took her by her arm and we led her into the master bedroom so she could help me choose the clothes to dress Olga María in, and the jewellery, and the right make-up, that's what I said, but Doña Olga, who's always so composed and together, was falling apart, she was sobbing, which is understandable, her eldest daughter, her most beloved daughter, was lying there dead in the living room, and for no reason whatsoever. I opened the closet door so we could look through her clothes, I was trying to distract Doña Olga; that's when I picked out that black-satin dress Olga María is wearing. I called Mercedes at the beauty salon to tell her what had happened and ask her to come to the funeral home to do

11

Olga María's hair as best she could, and I suggested Doña
Olga take away her daughter's jewellery, just in case the
policemen started rummaging through her things and
decided to steal whatever they could get their hands on.
The magistrate finally arrived just as we were leaving the
bedroom. Marito asked me to take Doña Olga to the
funeral home so she could be there when the body arrived
and help get it ready. So that's what I did. Then I went
home to change and make myself presentable once and
for all because I'm going to stay here all night – Diana is
arriving tomorrow morning, supposedly, that's Olga
María's younger sister, the one who's been living in Miami
for years, that's what she said, that she'd get on the first
flight tomorrow, they're three hours ahead, so there's no
way she could get here today. That one standing next to
the coffin must be Memo, Marito's second in command,
he just started working with him; Olga María didn't take
to him very well, probably because he took Julio Iglesias's
job – that's what we called the Spaniard who helped
Marito start the agency. Now, he was a hunk, tall and
gorgeous, though with a bit too much of a belly for my
taste, but he drove Olga María crazy for a few months,
that Julio Iglesias, she used to tell me she didn't know
what to do, he was her husband's partner, her husband's
friend, but she had the hots for him. It's not that she was
unfaithful, on the contrary, that's why it was so hard for
her, because that was the first time she'd been attracted in
that way to another man since she'd got married to Marito,
it was the first time she went further than being her

naturally flirtatious self, all Marito's fault, I can tell you, because this was when he'd all but abandoned Olga María. We never found out who was behind it – just look at him over there, all meek and mild-mannered, but Marito's a sneaky devil, I always suspected he had a few things on the side, and Olga María found out about at least two of his sluts. That was right around the time Marito decided to start his own agency, and he asked Julio Iglesias, from Madrid, also an expert in advertising, to be his partner; he'd just come to San Salvador as a consultant for the company Marito was working for. But I knew right off the bat: I'd seen that same gleam in Olga María's eyes when we were at the American School, when she started drooling over one of our classmates. Julio Iglesias began going over to their house for dinner, more and more frequently, and Olga María was getting hooked, little by little, because he liked her, too – who wouldn't? – and what with talking about the business and sitting around the table after dinner, they started finding opportunities to say things to each other, seducing each other right under Marito's nose, because he was putting all his energy into starting his agency. There was no applying the brakes once Julio Iglesias showed up one afternoon at the boutique, casually, as if he just happened to be at the Villas Españolas Mall to do a little shopping and just happened to run into a friend – his partner's wife – at her boutique. Olga María was totally nonchalant so Cheli and Conchita wouldn't notice that she was melting for that man who invited her out for a cup of coffee, right there, in the mall, and once they were sitting in the café he told her he couldn't stop thinking about her, he could no longer control his passion. And Olga María had to admit that she'd been thinking about him a lot, too, though she couldn't say she loved him, nor that she was in love with him, just that it was something weird, something new. Julio Iglesias had an apartment across the street from the Sheraton Hotel, near Villas Españolas; he suggested they meet there, that would be best, he didn't want to complicate things with Marito, his partner and friend. Olga María told him she'd give it some thought, it wasn't so simple, even though her relationship with Marito was on the rocks, she loved him, and there were the two girls, she didn't want to risk everything, throw away eleven years of her life. But Julio Iglesias kept at it: he called her at the boutique, came by every once in a while to invite her out for coffee (always making it seem proper, needless to say, even though Cheli and Conchita must have suspected something), and when he ate at the house he'd whisper sweet nothings in her ear. In the end she couldn't resist any longer and she said she would, she'd come to his apartment, but they had to plan it very carefully, there were lots of obstacles, because he couldn't pick her up at the boutique and she couldn't drive to his apartment – what if Marito or one of his friends saw her car parked in front of Julio Iglesias's apartment, how would they explain that, huh? That's where I came in, Auntie Laura, who else: best friend, confidante, the only one who could make this whole thing happen. You can't imagine, my dear, how nervous Olga María was at noon that day; the story was that I'd invited her out for lunch at a new vegetarian restaurant, so Marito should pick up the girls and then she'd go straight back to the boutique after lunch without going home. That was the story. The idea was that I'd pick her up at the boutique around twelve fifteen, then I'd drop her off at Julio Iglesias's apartment, I'd go eat lunch at my cousin's, and at two fifteen I'd pick her up. The poor thing was terrified when I got to the boutique – she was still hesitant; it was her first time. But as soon as we got in my car, she relaxed a little. She was dressed casually – a green miniskirt, I remember it perfectly – but very elegant, classy as usual. She stepped confidently out of the car, and I was the one left biting my fingernails, wondering how things were going, if finally they'd make love or if she'd only let him kiss her, she wasn't even sure herself. I'm telling you, that's the guy who took Julio Iglesias's place as vice president of Marito's advertising agency; look how the other employees greet him, with such respect, not at all like they treated that guy from Madrid I've been telling you about. Anyway, at two fifteen on the dot I was parked in front of Julio Iglesias's apartment; I honked the horn and saw her come out – happy, glowing, on cloud nine. I wanted her to tell me everything, all the juicy details, immediately. She told me she had the best time, better than she'd ever expected: he'd made a delicious salad and opened a fine bottle of white wine, ice cold – the way she loved it. He started kissing her the minute she stepped into the apartment, and he never stopped kissing and touching her, so tender, that's why she couldn't resist, and right there in the living room she let him undress her, and he kissed her all over her body so gently, a marvel, dear me – those were her very words. Then he picked her up and carried her to the bed, but the poor guy was kind of nervous, tense, so he came really fast, no warning, before they even got to the good stuff. Then he felt terrible, poor thing, and apologized. But that's no big deal, you know, my dear, it being the first time and all and with a man who caresses you so affectionately. That's what Olga María told me before I dropped her back off at the boutique. There's Sergio and Cuca now. Sergio's a handsome devil, I can't figure out how he ended up with Cuca, even though she is nice, but she's not woman enough for him, don't you think? The problem was that Julio Iglesias started to fall in love. The second time – I dropped Olga María off at his apartment another afternoon – not only did he declare his love and tell her he was thinking about her constantly but also that he wanted her to be his for ever, she should divorce Marito, it didn't make sense for her to stay with him if she didn't love him any more, he wanted to marry her and give her everything she could ever want, on the spot, right then and there. Can you imagine? My dear, men really are brutes: there he had her all to himself, ready and willing, to be enjoyed to his heart's content, but no, he had to start in with his demands, with all that possessiveness nonsense, as if Olga María would be fool enough to leave Marito, the father of her children, just for the sake of going off to live with some Spaniard. That

Julio Iglesias turned out to be a real cretin: he was so obsessed he didn't even care that Marito was his partner and friend, he called her with no discretion whatsoever, and then he'd show up at the boutique acting like a lunatic. That's why there never was a third time. Olga María got desperate, being stalked like that, with such pig-headedness: she asked him not to call her any more, to forget about what had happened between them. She reminded him she was a married woman and had two daughters – he couldn't just ignore all that – and she told him there was absolutely no way she would leave Marito to live with him. You know what that dimwit said? My dear, he said he had a flat and a Mercedes Benz in Madrid and she could start a new life there, they could just slip away so there wouldn't even be a scandal. Yes, my dear, handsome but dumb, that Julio Iglesias. He finally calmed down, resigned himself to the situation, but not before trying to blackmail her – can you believe it? – he threatened to tell Marito. A few months ago he went back to Madrid for good. He and Olga María were distant, cold, civil to each other when Marito was around – and as it turned out Julio Iglesias was nothing but a sham, he had a wife in Spain and a few weeks after his *affaire*, as they say, with Olga María, he fell head over heels in love with some accountant who worked in the agency. That's what I'm telling you: you can never trust a man. He even tried to seduce me, the brute. He was still going on about how much in love he was with Olga María – and then he leapt at the first opportunity to ask me over for dinner, with the excuse that he wanted to talk about her. I wasn't buying a word of it, my dear. The way he looked at me when he asked me over, and then again, at a soirée at Olga María's, let's just say it wasn't exactly the way you look at your confidante. But he was very handsome, that Julio Iglesias, so I played along. He told me he wanted me to see his apartment; after all, we could speak freely there, and he promised to whip up a fettuccine al pesto, his own special recipe. He's a really good cook, my dear. I made it clear from the get-go that the only reason I'd accepted his invitation was my friendship with Olga María. I swear, the minute I entered his apartment, I didn't let him change the subject; I asked him what Olga María thought of his furniture, the pictures on the walls, the decor in general. I hung out with him in the kitchen, because he hadn't finished cooking, and he poured me a glass of delicious Rioja, then he started rattling on about his great love for Olga María, his passion, the most amazing thing he'd experienced in El Salvador; he even rolled his eyes, that Julio Iglesias, when he repeated that nonsense about how he was willing to do anything to save his relationship with her. Yes, my dear, men are disgusting. Just imagine, when afterwards I found out he was already going out with the accountant from the agency. But that evening in his apartment he was playing the same old tape: Olga María's indifference was killing him, I needed to help him, convince Olga María to get back together with him. I just let him talk; the wine was delicious and so was the dinner. It was during dessert when I told him I was envious of the

18

intensity of his love for Olga María, nobody was in love with me that way. Why did I say that, my dear? Suddenly, he changed: he was quiet for a moment, then he started playing a new tape, and now it was as if Olga María had never existed, he started off saying he couldn't believe me, he absolutely couldn't believe that somebody wasn't deeply in love with a woman like me, he'd noticed how beautiful I was the first time he saw me, but he'd always thought I looked down on him or just wasn't interested. He took off from there, my dear, seducing me, absolutely shamelessly, not even taking into account the fact that I'd come to his apartment to talk about his relationship with Olga María, and pretty soon he was brushing up against me, flirting, whispering things in my ear, holding my hand, trying to kiss me. But I didn't let him, no, my dear, I didn't. I told him to behave himself. But he kept pushing himself on me – so pig-headed. At one point he almost managed to kiss me. That's when I stood up and told him I was leaving, he wasn't showing me any respect. To tell you the truth, though, that Julio Iglesias was gorgeous, and I was really tempted to let him have his way with me, and maybe, my dear, he read my mind, because he sure didn't put on the brakes, he just kept insisting. Men are not to be trusted. That's why I divorced Alberto, and I have no regrets: it's the best thing I could have done, and I said as much to Olga María at the time: it isn't worth complicating your life, it's better to be with one man or none at all. I'm glad they've already started serving coffee, my throat is dry, and I'm so exhausted I'm afraid I'm going to collapse.

Pass me a cup. If you want, let's go out on the terrace for some fresh air. There are so many cars parked in front and half the people haven't even arrived. This place will be packed later tonight, my dear, with everybody from the advertising world and Sergio's friends from the association of travel agencies. I wonder how many of our classmates from the American School will show up. It's been so long since we had a class reunion. Chele Yuca will show up, that's for sure, considering how in love with Olga María he's always been. You know him, don't you? His first name is Gastón: he was the handsomest boy in our class. Did you see my mother? She's standing next to the coffin talking with Alberto. Those two always got along well. I don't know how my mother can stand him. No, my dear, I've got nothing to say to him; we were married for a year, and in that time we said everything we had to say to each other – and there was plenty of time left over. Alberto is the most boring man you can imagine. I don't know how I managed to put up with him for a whole year. He's always at his computer, for hours and hours, the whole day if he doesn't have anything better to do. It can drive you to despair, my dear, he doesn't want to go out, or meet people, or go to the movies – it's atrocious. I practically had to drag him out to dinner parties. But my mother says he's very intelligent and that's why his business is doing so well, and she says he's the most knowledgeable person in the country not only about finances but about everything that's going on in the world, and that's why he has so much money, all her friends assure her that he's the number-one financial consultant. As far as I'm concerned, let him make all the money he wants, my dear, let him go to Wall Street with his computers for all I care, but don't let him dare get anywhere near me – he's like the plague, he infects you with boredom in a matter of seconds. The problem is that my mother still doesn't accept the fact that we're divorced, she just can't understand how someone can send a man packing who makes that much money, even if he does bore you to tears; as far as she's concerned, you're supposed to live with the same man your whole life. No, my dear, I'm not going to change her this late in the game. I guarantee you, the moment she hears I'm going to marry someone else, she's going to come to me with a ton of objections, unless, that is, he's got more money than Alberto. Olga María didn't believe it either when I told her I was divorcing Alberto, I told her I couldn't stand him any more, I'd rather go back and live with my parents than be so unbearably bored any longer. She told me not to leave him – our problem was we didn't have any children. Can you imagine? I wasn't about to have kids with somebody like that. Pure madness. No, I don't think my father will come: he's at the finca dealing with endless problems. Now that I see what he has to deal with, I'm convinced Doña Olga did the right thing to sell the fincas Don Sergio left her. Owning coffee plantations isn't what it used to be, there's one setback after another these days, first the communists taking them over and not allowing the harvest, and now the drop in prices. It never ends, my dear. That's why Doña Olga did the right thing to sell, it was for the best. My father should do the same, and I've told him so, but he's pig-headed, attached to his land. Hey, look who just arrived. I can't believe it, it's José Carlos, that crazy photographer, I thought he'd already left the country, what a surprise. He was working at Marito's agency until a few weeks ago. He takes beautiful photographs, a real artist; he studied in Boston, then stayed there for a few years and took photos of famous artists, of afternoons on the beach and in forests, of old buildings. He published a book of his photographs: Olga María showed it to me, inscribed with a poem José Carlos wrote to her. He'll be going back to Boston in a few days. He could only stand this country for a year. He says he's bored here. Just look at him, all scrawny and awkward-looking, but still, there's something attractive about him. Olga María went out with him, for only a few weeks, but enough to get to know him. It was sort of the same story: Marito and José Carlos went to grammar school and high school together at the San José Externado, best friends growing up, until the war, then they each took a different path, but as soon as José Carlos decided to return, Marito offered him a job at the agency, and they became thick as thieves again. So José Carlos started coming over to their house frequently, whenever he felt like it, and he got to be better friends with Olga María, it was only to be expected, she was the wife of his best friend and they already knew each other, though not too well, from school. For Olga María it was a revelation of sorts. José Carlos is so laid-back, kind of wacky, he's got all kinds of exotic ideas, even sort of half-communist ideas sometimes. At first, she wasn't attracted to him physically, but little by little she realized how amazing the guy was, he knew about so many things, one of those super-sensitive artist types, he's travelled all over the world, been part of the artistic *milieu* in the States. That's what Olga María told me. There it was again, that gleam in her eyes I was telling you about, that same gleam I saw when we were at the American School, that she got whenever she'd start to get interested in a classmate, the same gleam I saw with that Julio Iglesias. I couldn't quite fathom that my friend could be interested in such a bizarre-looking guy. You wouldn't have believed it either, would you? Look at him over there: in blue jeans and a sports shirt at a wake, no jacket, only he would do something like that. I'll introduce him to you a little later so you can see that he's a little off his rocker. I admit he could be interesting as a friend – it's always like that with artists – but not to fall in love with. It was just like what happened with Julio Iglesias, there came a moment when Olga María decided to visit José Carlos's studio, but this time she didn't need me to give her a ride because she had the perfect excuse: José Carlos was going to take a series of photographs of her to include in his next exhibition. That's what she told Marito, and me, too. But I already knew what she was going for. José Carlos did take some gorgeous pictures of her – very suggestive – for what it's worth: in the pictures Olga María is made up in an oriental style and she's wearing nothing but a semi-transparent silk tunic, and she's carrying exotic-looking crucifixes of some kind and is surrounded by mirrors. It was hard for me to get her to tell me what was going on, because during that period, for a number of reasons, but especially because of her constant visits to José Carlos's studio, we barely saw each other. I was afraid Olga María was going to fall in love, get herself mixed up in some mess she wouldn't be able to get herself out of. I told her it was none of my business and I didn't want to stick my nose in where it didn't belong, but she should be careful, take it easy, take more precautions, I reminded her it wasn't in her best interests that Marito find out what was going on or even suspect anything. One afternoon, finally, I found her at the boutique, and she invited me out for a cup of coffee and told me not to worry, her relationship with José Carlos wasn't going to go any further, she was sure of that. She liked him a lot, but she could never live with someone like that, he was too unstable, and she told me that even he was aware of that and from the get-go he'd told her straight out that he loved being with her, making love with her, but that was all – he would never take his best friend's wife away nor was he in any position to live with her and the two girls. Hearing that reassured me, and that same afternoon Olga María showed me the first photographs José Carlos had taken of her, and she told me he was very professional – he'd made her pose for several hours and, when he finished shooting, he took her to bed – and a great lover, not like that Julio Iglesias, who shot his wad before the word go. But you know what men are like, my dear, don't you? Turns out a month later, Olga

María completely lost interest, and out of the blue she
told José Carlos that enough was enough, she wanted to
end their relationship, Marito was getting suspicious, and
she wasn't willing to take any more chances, it would be
better for them to stop seeing each other, and they should
just be friends like before. And that's when José Carlos
lost his head. It's like I told you: you can never trust
anybody or predict anything. He started going on about
how much he was in love with her and there wasn't any
reason for them to stop seeing each other – he'd never had
a relationship like that, he'd never fallen in love with a
woman like her or in that way, so intensely, he'd never
experienced such intimacy. Can you believe it, my dear?
He was the one who said it was only about sex with
friendship, and now here he was, singing Julio Iglesias's
same tune: he was willing to give up everything for her, he
even suggested the stupid idea that they go live in Boston
together, the girls would get a better education there. But
she put her foot down, she told him in no uncertain terms
to cut the crap, there was nothing between them any more,
she had no regrets, she'd had a great time in bed, and she
was grateful for the pictures, but he should get it into his
head that their relationship was over, finished. One thing
was different, though, one way he wasn't at all like Julio
Iglesias, and that was the way they each got over their
heartbreak. You know what I mean? José Carlos, maybe
because he's an artist, I don't know, or whatever, he
couldn't get over being in love with her, even though he
stopped calling her and almost stopped visiting her (he

went to their house only a few more times – mostly for business dinners – and only after Marito insisted that his best friend and star employee show up). He had a chip on his shoulder, as if Olga María had cheated him, emotionally, and whenever he saw her he put on this pathetic expression, like he was the victim, the innocent babe she'd taken advantage of. That's when he started saying he was going back to Boston, he was bored in this country, he had contributed everything he could to Marito's agency. I told Olga María that José Carlos's little song and dance about returning to Boston was nothing more than a subtle kind of blackmail, his way of complaining that she'd forsaken him, she never paid any attention to him any more. Olga María agreed with me, and she was so naughty she even got it into her head to throw José Carlos a goodbye party, a surprise party, this was about three weeks ago, but I think he smelt a rat, and when Marito invited him for dinner on that Saturday – just to chat about his work at the agency – José Carlos made up some excuse, said he was working on a project of his own that he wanted to finish before leaving for Boston, lunch the following week would be better, because he was busy every night, trying to be disciplined and work on his art. No, my dear, Olga María's plan didn't pan out, but that would have been something, don't you think? Now he looks very upset, poor guy, just look at his face, he really was in love with her, he'll be better off going back to Boston and taking all his strange notions with him. I'm sure he was involved with the subversives, even though he does come from a good family, just goes to show what those Jesuit priests did to some of those boys, a lot of Marito and José Carlos's classmates ended up being terrorists – those priests brainwashed them, indoctrinated them. They say José Carlos went to the States so he wouldn't get killed, his parents sent him away when they realized he was mixed up in shady goings-on, that's why he didn't come back until the war was over – he was afraid. Olga María told me José Carlos never talked about politics, he spent all his time in the States working and studying, but as you know, my dear, in this place, everybody knows everything about everybody, and I heard he was involved with one of those solidarity committees, taking photographs and working with them. I wouldn't be at all surprised. Now it's really getting crowded, so many people I don't know. Any minute now Doña Olga will arrive with the girls, those poor dears, so young and they've already lost their mother. It's going to be very difficult for Marito, he was such a good husband, but Olga María deserved him, she was also totally devoted to him, it was a two-way street, she never complained much, not even when she heard the rumours about him and one of his secretaries, Olga María was always so discreet, so modest, so reserved, never had those fits of hysteria, she defended her home and was totally devoted to her husband and children, that's why her death makes me so angry, my dear, what's the point, so many bastards they don't bother killing and a woman like that – a paragon, so hard-working, look how she started that boutique from scratch, with her own hard work. Those two coming in now, they're the two policemen who came to Doña Olga's to harass us, the one with the dark jacket is the one who says his name is Deputy Chief Handal: riff-raff, my dear, they've got no respect for other people's pain, what's wrong with these people, how dare they come to a decent person's wake, their heads must be full of rot – imagine: they wanted me to reveal all of Olga María's secrets, as if any of her friends or acquaintances would have arranged her murder – they even suspect Marito. I think it was simply a mistake, or most likely a thief who got nervous and didn't know what to do, so he shot her, it wouldn't be the first time that's happened, a fiend like that, the only thing he knows how to do is kill people. Nobody I know would have been capable of even imagining doing Olga María any harm, it wouldn't have crossed anybody's mind to even think badly of her, such a good woman, so generous, she never stuck her nose into other people's business. Look, here come Doña Olga and the girls, let's go, come with me, they look so lovely, they're going to sit next to their daddy, they are the apples of Doña Olga's eyes, her only two granddaughters, because Sergio and Cuca – I'm pretty sure – they can't have children, and Diana is still too young and who knows what kind of life she leads in Miami, you know how those gringas are, women there don't necessarily have kids right away any more, and Diana's practically a gringa, she's been there almost twelve years. I hope that brute Handal doesn't think he's going to interrogate the girls here, then I really would get mad, they've got no right; anyway what are they doing here instead of out looking for the murderer, they have the description little Olga gave them, what more do they want? What infuriates me most is that in the end, I bet you, they won't catch anybody – they're so incompetent, it'd be a miracle if they did. When have you ever seen the police catch anybody who is truly guilty of anything? Never. I didn't even notice when dear Julita arrived, probably right after Doña Olga and the girls, but with all these people I must've missed her. Our Julita is so good, so trustworthy, she loved Olga María more than anything, like her own daughter, she took care of her for twenty years, can you imagine, that's a lifetime. She came to their house when Olga María was ten years old, from a little Indian village, Tacuba, way out there in Ahuachapán. You can't find servants like that any more, I'm telling you, my dear, everything has changed so much, now they're all prostitutes and thieves, or both – you can't leave the house alone for a minute because they'll ransack it. Horrible, my dear, you can't trust anybody any more, even if they do have references and recommendations, they're always up to some mischief. That was a different world: servants used to be part of the family, like our dear Julita, who is now going to have to finish raising little Olga and Raquelita; Marito will need her now more than ever, and Doña Olga will, too. That's what I told Julita this afternoon. The poor thing must be very distraught, but you know how Indians are, you can't tell what they're feeling, with that face they've got, like a mask. Hey, I told you, and I was right: look who just arrived, my dear,

Gastón Berrenechea himself, the one and only Yuca, look how handsome he is, and just as charming as ever, always so elegant, look how impeccably dressed, in that suit with that tie, beautiful, I've never seen that design in black; I swear, at the American School we all thought Yuca and Olga María were going to get married, they would have made the perfect couple, both so good-looking, as if they were made for each other, but they only went out for a few months, such a pity, we couldn't understand why it didn't last, but even then Yuca was too much of a womanizer – unmanageable. I met both of them even before that, can you believe it, my dear, about twenty years ago, even more, twenty-three years ago, when we started first grade, it's been for ever and a day. Now Yuca is a VIP, you know, he owns a chain of superstores, and he's a deputy in the government and a high-ranking party official, it's so weird, I never thought Yuca would end up in politics, they're even pushing him as a candidate for president, my dear, but he's still pretty young, he's still got to earn his stripes. You know he married Kati, Don Federico Schultz's daughter, filthy rich, they're drowning in money, and she's the apple of Don Federico's eye; it's largely due to Don Federico that Yuca has done so well. He's supported him in everything, not only in business – starting up that superstore chain – but also in politics, he's treated him like a son, without Don Federico's support who knows how poor Yuca would have ended up, my dear, his family lost almost everything during the agrarian reform, what a disgrace, the Berrenecheas were the richest cotton growers in the country, but those communists with their agrarian reform pretty much left them penniless, practically in the streets. That's what I mean when I say Yuca owes so much to Don Federico, there are even people who say terrible things about how Yuca married Kati for the money, people are so spiteful, my dear, and now that he's a politician they just want to sling mud at him. Yuca is a very hard worker, you've got to give it to him, and if he got involved in politics it was because they took all his family's fincas, I remember it well, my dear, right at the beginning of the war, Yuca was up there with the old man Le Chevalier, taking a stand against the communists. He hasn't had anything handed to him on a silver platter, on the contrary, that man has worked like a dog to get where he is, that's why Don Federico lent him a hand. Quite a man, Yuca: nice, good-looking, intelligent. He'll be president in about five years, definitely, no doubt about it, his rise is meteoric, he's getting more and more popular all the time. He's got loads of charisma, my dear, people will vote for him, people like to have a leader who's successful, in business, I mean, someone who knows how to speak in public, and it's even better if he's handsome, even very handsome like Yuca. He's so different from that idiot we have for president now, that stupid fat old man, his own mother doesn't even like him, I voted for him just so the communists wouldn't win. Imagine what a terrible situation, my dear: we had to choose between that fanatic and the communists. With Yuca it would be different; he's so distinguished. You just saw him: nice, don't you think?

31

He'd have as much pull as old Le Chevalier, people simply adore him. The communists are already afraid of him, that's why they've started a campaign to try to discredit him, saying he was a member of the death squads, he put bombs in some ministry or other during the agrarian reform – the same old accusations – he's taken advantage of his contacts with people in the government to make millions off those superstores – the same nonsense they pull out of their hats whenever they want to ruin an honourable person. I really like Yuca, my dear, I always did, ever since we were small, at the American School, and Olga María did, too, even though all they ever did was say hi when they ran into each other at the Club, their teenage romance already long forgotten, but even though they'd both got married, made separate lives for themselves, and taken different paths, Yuca always carried a torch for Olga María, I'm absolutely sure of it, and Olga María always carried a torch for him, that's why I wasn't at all surprised three months ago when she told me she saw him again, apparently they ran into each other in the parking lot of the Villas Españolas Mall; as usual she was rushing to the boutique, and he was surrounded by his bodyguards on his way to pick up a suit at Chaín the Turk's shop. I could see it in her eyes as she was talking about him, she had that same gleam I already told you about. I didn't want to ask her too much about it, my dear, because Yuca is so important, but I understood that the two of them had left something unfinished from fifteen years ago, having been boyfriend-girlfriend as teenagers, just kissing and touching, but no sex, something that now, who knows why, they decided to finish. The problem was, how to meet: Yuca's always surrounded by bodyguards – a big show of security, what with all the kidnappings, my dear, it's a good thing, and anyway both of them being married and all. It wasn't easy. For days on end all they could do was talk on the phone, just waiting for their chance. Olga María was excited, she was acting like a teenager, she wanted him so badly, she wanted to be with Yuca, but at the same time she was afraid of getting into trouble, not only with Marito and Kati, but because of Yuca's political activities, he has a lot of enemies, even in his own party and the government, and you know how dirty politics can be, my dear, which is why Olga María was afraid her relationship with him would be used against him by his enemies or to blackmail her, these days nobody feels safe. So, surprise surprise, my dear, what do you know? It was Aunt Laura once again to the rescue, so once and for all Olga María could get together with Yuca, so they could abandon themselves to their passions, do whatever they had to do. One afternoon I picked her up at Villas Españolas and drove her to a secret hideaway in Miramonte, where Yuca was waiting for her. She was superexcited, and she looked gorgeous. I came back to pick her up two hours later. She was totally disappointed – she barely answered my questions, in monosyllables. I figured Yuca must not have been at the top of his game. I kept at her to tell me the details, like she always had before, after all, that's what I was her friend for, if you know what I mean. But Olga María said she'd rather not talk about it. There was a second time, another afternoon, I took her to the same house under the same circumstances. This time she wasn't quite so excited, even though she was all gussied up and happy, but like someone who's determined not to go getting her hopes up. When she came out, she was even more disappointed than the time before, and again she kept quiet, she'd tell me later when we had more time, she promised. In the end she did, even though she still didn't want to tell me many details: she kept repeating that she and Yuca were incompatible, something wasn't working right, she'd completely lost interest. I asked her what Yuca thought about it. She told me he wanted them to keep seeing each other, he didn't want to give her up, he said he was madly in love with her, they should keep trying, the same story as with the other two. But you can see how Olga María was, my dear, in her sweet, gentle way she had quite a strong personality – when she said no, she meant no. Poor Yuca was being stood up: there he was, all dressed up and nowhere to go, that's why I told you he couldn't *not* show up at the wake, because he's been in love with Olga María ever since grammar school, and he must be suffering from her death more than almost anybody. But now the place is really full, my dear, let's go say hello to some people, we don't want anybody to think badly of us, as if we came to Olga María's wake just to gossip. Follow me, I'll introduce you first of all to José Carlos.

2. The Burial

How horribly hot it was in that church, my dear. I can't figure out why they decided to hold the funeral so early in the day. They really should have air conditioning in churches. This isn't the first time I've thought of that: if those priests installed air conditioning, I swear we'd come to church more often. I told my mother that the last time I went, and she made a face like you wouldn't believe, like I was committing blasphemy. Good thing we're in the car now and that I parked it in the shade. For a moment there I was sweating so much I thought my make-up would run. What a talkative priest, my dear. But let's just wait here until the air conditioning kicks in – I've been sweating so much I feel like dashing home and taking a shower instead of following in the funeral procession. I'm going to join in behind Sergio and Cuca. Sergio's car is such a pretty colour, I love that lilac; I wanted one that colour but BMW doesn't make it, only Toyota, so I chose white, because it goes with everything and I wasn't about to buy a different make just because there wasn't lilac. Some people don't care; Alberto, my ex-husband, is like that. I've had only BMWs for about twelve years now, ever since Papa gave me my first car when I turned eighteen and entered the university. I remember celebrating with Olga María. A day that started out beautiful and ended up ugly. The day after the graduation party, there it was, the car, parked in front of our house. It was a total surprise, and I was ecstatic. I called all my friends from school and told them to come over and see it: BMW, latest model, crimson red. I drove around in it the whole day with Olga María and some other friends. Papa warned me not to drive too fast, but once we decided to drive to the port and we were out on the highway, I floored it. Poor Olga María, we were so happy that day, and now, look at her, ahead of us in that hearse. I still can't believe it. That same night I was showing off my BMW, we also had a brush with death; that's why I'm remembering it now, you can't imagine what a horrible experience it was. We went to the Zona Rosa to have a few beers and hang out with some friends. You won't believe it, but we'd just left Chilli's, and we were walking to the corner where I'd left my car and suddenly there was a shoot-out. All hell broke loose. A bunch of terrorists suddenly appeared out of nowhere and started shooting some gringos sitting on the terrace of the Mediterraneo Restaurant. You can't believe the panic. Everybody threw themselves on the ground and started shouting their heads off, because the shooting seemed to last for ever. I tore my brand-new blue jeans, right on the knee, and Olga María almost broke her wrist. It was dreadful. When the shooting stopped, there was this deathly silence, and we all slowly crept over to where the gringos were all shot up. They killed them all; there were about ten of them sprawled out on the floor, bleeding like pigs. Dreadful, my dear, really gruesome. We'd just walked by there no more than a minute earlier. Isn't that incredible, that nothing happened to us then and now Olga María ended up dying like this? I swear, we almost had a fit of hysteria. I don't know how we managed to find our way to the car and get out of there. Two of the gringos were really handsome. I remember perfectly how they stared at Olga María and me when we walked past their table. That's what we were talking about – hard as it is to believe, even if it seems like I'm making this up – about how hot two of those gringos were, when suddenly the shooting started. I hate driving in funeral processions. Other people hate you, it causes huge traffic jams and it makes me feel like I'm on display in a shop window. If Olga María hadn't been such a good friend, I'd have driven straight to the cemetery and not followed the hearse – that's what I usually do when it isn't someone this close. Hand me that Miguel Bosé cassette. He's so hot. I love him. Finally, the air conditioning is starting to work. I don't know why that hearse is going so slowly. It's practically standing still. What's going on? Maybe it's because there are too many of us. This must be one of the longest processions there's been in a long time – Olga María and Marito's families are so well known; well, to tell the truth, Olga María's is more. By the way, did you notice how gorgeous Diana looked? She looks so much like Olga María, a Xerox copy. Miami's climate suits her. I'd love to have a tan like that. But the sun here is too harsh: it just burns you, turns you into a boiled shrimp, and then the tan doesn't last at all. Things are going really well for Diana in Miami. We had a long talk this morning. I told her exactly what happened.

She suspects there's more than meets the eye. She said she has no intention of standing around twiddling her thumbs, she's even considering hiring a gringo private detective to come here and investigate; she doesn't trust the police here at all. I don't either, especially that Deputy Chief Handal, what an oaf. Did I tell you he started interrogating me this afternoon? Stupid idiot. He wants me to tell him all of Olga María's most intimate secrets just so he can confirm his own filthy suspicions. He even threatened me, if I didn't cooperate, he'd get a subpoena. Please, do me a favour! Ask me whatever you want, I told him, once and for all, but I warned him, I'm only going to answer the questions I feel like answering. And you know what he asked? If I knew of any life-insurance policies Marito had taken out on Olga María. I told him these aren't things decent people go around talking about, every respectable family has life-insurance policies of course. Please, do me a favour. That Deputy Chief Handal is a boor – instead of looking for the murderer, he spends his time digging into Olga María's family life. I told him: Don't be so vile! What, I said to him, are you trying to insinuate that Mario hired somebody to kill Olga María so he could get her life insurance? What a vile insinuation – and I, for one, wasn't going to put up with it. He said I shouldn't misunderstand, he was only trying to verify information he'd got elsewhere and he wasn't by any stretch of the imagination suggesting that Mr Trabanino had hired somebody to kill his wife. That's what that cretin said: "Mr Trabanino". Then he really threw me for a loop. You know what he asked me? If I knew what kind of relationship there'd been between Olga María and Gastón Berrenechea, the lawyer. Now, why would he ask me that? We were in the reception room at the funeral home, it was almost empty, but everyone must have heard me shouting at him to stop being so impertinent, show some respect for the dead, get out of here immediately unless he wanted me to get Olga María's relatives to throw him out. Can you imagine such an outrage? I bet he was a terrorist, or something like it, during the war. Well, with this new police force they put together after they signed that peace treaty with the communists, you never know. I am absolutely positive that Handal is working with Yuca's enemies. You've got to be very careful with people of that ilk. Can you imagine the scandal if the press got wind of Yuca's *affaire* with Olga María! I get chills just thinking about it: it would be the end of his entire political career. What a weird route the driver of that hearse is taking. I would have turned left here: it makes more sense – why does he want to go all the way through Colonia San Francisco? He should've turned there and gone through Colonia San Mateo. I love this song by Miguel Bosé, especially the part where he whistles. Whose car did Diana go in? Oh, she's with Marito and Doña Olga and the girls. And Julita? I didn't see her. She's probably in Sergio and Cuca's car. Or maybe they had her stay and watch over the house; I doubt it, though. I was worried about that Deputy Chief Handal starting to poke his nose into the relationship between Olga María and Yuca. I should warn Yuca. I'll find a chance at the cemetery.

How could Handal have found out about it if Olga María and I were the only ones who knew? I don't think even Julita realized it, and even if she did, she'd never tell, especially not somebody like him. The only possibility is that one of the girls from the boutique – Cheli or Conchita – blabbed. I'm going to warn them: they shouldn't talk to that policeman. I hate having to change gears every other minute, and the motor gets overheated when you drive this slowly. I don't understand why there aren't any cemeteries in any decent parts of the city – do you, my dear? They're all so far away, so out of the way, and always in the middle of dangerous neighbourhoods. Well, the truth is, this city's contaminated with slums. That's what Diana told me, it always surprises her how the neighbourhoods where decent people live are practically surrounded by slums – where the criminals come from. That's why it's so easy to get murdered without anybody being able to do anything about it, like what happened to Olga María: the criminals do their dirty work, then quickly sneak back to their hideouts. In other cities it's not like that: you live on one side and the bad guys live on the other, and there's miles in between, which is how it should be. But in this country, everything's all squished together. Olga María showed me how just as you enter her neighbourhood, right next to the slums, there are three row houses up against one another, wall to wall: in one there's a grammar school, the next one's a whore house, and in the next one there's an evangelical church. Can you imagine!? Sheer madness. This stop light is going to break up the procession. We're going to lose each other. It takes for ever for the light to turn green. We should have had a police escort to stop the traffic; I don't know why nobody thought of hiring a policeman – that disgusting Deputy Chief Handal could be doing that instead of sticking his nose into things that are none of his business. The good part is that from here on out, once we're on the highway, there won't be much traffic, until we get close to the cemetery, that is, then the streets get horrible, super-narrow. Diana said she's going to be here for only three days; she can't stay longer, because of her job, she's a top executive at some computer company with its head-quarters in Miami, and she's finishing up her Master's in Business Administration. That girl's really talented. She's three years younger than me and Olga María. Don Sergio sent her there for high school and then she just stayed on in Miami. She comes to visit from time to time, at the most once a year, especially since Don Sergio died; she'd rather Doña Olga come to her because she can rest there. She was asking me about what Olga María had been up to recently; they weren't in contact much, according to her. I'm not going to go telling her everything Olga María didn't tell her; I don't want to stick my foot in my mouth. She especially wanted to know if I suspect anyone in particular, if I can think of anyone who might have arranged the murder, because as far as she's concerned it was a contract killing, arranged by somebody who had a strong motive to get rid of Olga María. She kept insisting, I'm telling you, my dear, almost like that Deputy Chief

Handal, wanting me to tell her what I thought. I told her the truth, that I'm pretty confused about everything myself. I don't know anybody who could have even thought about committing such a brutal crime – maybe it was a mistake. But Diana said it couldn't have been a mistake, the murderer was waiting specifically for Olga María, he knew who he was killing. What if it was a way of sending a message to Marito? I wondered out loud. Why did I say that, tell me?! Because then Diana started interrogating me as if I knew something. I told her I didn't, it was just a guess that popped into my head. Can you imagine if I'd told her about Olga María's relationships with José Carlos and Yuca? Who knows what she would have imagined! She's very upset, the poor thing. Anybody would be in her situation. Here we are at the roundabout; let's see if from here to El Ranchón the driver of the hearse will step on it a little. We're going so slowly. But what worries me most is this business with Yuca, because that Deputy Chief Handal is already making all kinds of conjectures. I care about Yuca, a lot, and he really trusts me. I mean, when his relationship with Olga María wasn't working out and she didn't want to tell me any details, it was Yuca himself who filled me in. The poor guy was really down, almost desperate. He called me at home and said he needed to see me, urgently. I already knew what it was about, but I was still surprised because Yuca hadn't called me for years, ever since he got involved in politics and married Kati. We were pretty good friends before that, I even dated him for a while. I never told you? Yes.

Nothing ever happened, but we went out several times. That's why I wasn't totally surprised when I got a call from him. At first I thought I should talk to Olga María before seeing Yuca, but then I told myself that if she hadn't wanted to tell me anything, it was better not to insist. We agreed that the following afternoon I'd go to his house in Miramonte, where he'd taken Olga María. Look for that José María cassette, I love that Spanish singer. Have you heard him? I found poor Yuca so changed – handsome, as usual, but politics ages people, my dear. It's a pity. But what was most noticeable was his level of anxiety. He couldn't sit still. Every other second he was standing up, pacing around, calling someone on his cell phone, talking to someone on his walkie-talkie. I figured Yuca used that house as some kind of secret office. He and I were the only ones inside, but outside, in the garden and the garage, there were about half a dozen bodyguards. From the minute I got there he started telling me about how I needed to convince Olga María to see him again, how I was her best friend and only I could make that happen, how he would be for ever grateful to me if I did. He didn't even wait for me to sit down, get comfortable on the sofa; he didn't even offer me something to drink, he just launched right into his tirade about what I should tell Olga María – it was like he was possessed. I told him to calm down and get me something to drink, I asked him if he'd totally forgotten his manners, I told him to please remember who I was, Laura, remember me? Not some messenger-girl, so please get off his high horse. That's when he offered me a whiskey and poured another for himself, but not just a regular shot, more like a full half-glass, and he downed it in one gulp. I realized he was really in bad shape, he needed help. I asked what the hell was going on with him; I asked him to please calm down, have a seat, relax. These are the streets I was talking about that I don't like. What's this called? Colonia Costa Rica? Are you sure? I know my way here, I've come here so often to bury people, but I've never known what it's called. After you go under that bridge you can see the cemetery. I have no idea how to get to the main cemetery, the one downtown; I get lost in that part of town, but I don't think they bury anybody there any more, my dear. As I was saying, Yuca sort of calmed down. I told him I couldn't do anything for him unless he told me in detail what had happened between him and Olga María. I warned him not to give me any cock-and-bull stories, to tell me the truth, the whole truth, and nothing but the truth. He looked a little taken aback: he thought Olga María had already told me everything. I said she hadn't, I said she was a very discreet woman, and she'd only told me that things hadn't worked out between them. Then Yuca asked me to wait a second, he had to go to the bathroom, and off he dashed. What a mess this is, my dear. We're at a standstill. That's what I hate about these narrow streets, the tiniest thing goes wrong and there's a major traffic jam. We could sit here now for fifteen minutes. That's happened to me before. It's because right after the bridge the street gets even narrower, sometimes the hearse can't even get through. What a pain. But I was telling you about Yuca – I do feel like it's somehow wrong to talk about it: it's so private. Especially considering Yuca's political position, my dear, it might be embarrassing, even dangerous. But I think he's doing better. He looks good now, more relaxed, stable, self-assured, not like that afternoon I was with him in his hideout. When he got back from the bathroom he was acting totally different: like he was having tremors. Then I understood what was going on with him, and I got scared, why not admit it. A man of his stature in a situation like that, it's enough to frighten anyone. So, again, I told him to relax, I suggested he have a seat on the sofa next to me and tell me what had happened with Olga María. First, he gave me a whole long song and dance: about how he'd always loved her, how she was the best thing in his life, how he needed such a sweet, understanding woman by his side, how his relationship with Kati was dead. You know: what men always say to women. I let him go on for a while, but when I realized he was beating around the bush, I asked him point blank why Olga María had entered that house so excited and exited it so disappointed. Yuca was sitting next to me on the sofa. He didn't answer, he looked me right in the eyes and began caressing my hair, with the saddest expression on his face. I felt sorry for him, and he knew how to use that to his advantage, he knows I've always liked him. He inched closer and closer, a little bit at a time, then he kissed me. The weird part is that I didn't do anything to stop him. On the contrary. It was as if I had the feeling that this was the only way I was going to get this man to settle down, the only way I was going to find out what had really happened between him and Olga María. Anyway, that's the only way I can explain it, and to tell you the truth, once we started, it didn't seem like we were going to stop. Yuca is so good-looking, so tender; he knows how to say such lovely things. And his body, my dear, if you ordered one custom made, it wouldn't turn out better than his. But the more we kissed and touched each other on the sofa, the more frantic he got. He told me he loved my legs, he wanted to lick me all over. He almost tore my clothes off. I came there totally defenceless: I was wearing a grey plaid miniskirt and a white blouse. I had no idea that man was going to throw himself on me like that; if I'd known, I'd have worn pants. I managed to tell him to be careful or he'd tear my stockings, but he was totally beside himself; all he wanted to do was bury his head between my legs, like a dog. I managed to grab him by the hair and shout at him to calm down, I didn't like it like that – now I understood why Olga María had been so disappointed in him; I asked him what it would take for him to go about it a little more gently. Poor Yuca. I still get an odd feeling when I remember the look on his face. He was on his knees on the floor and I'd already stood up. He rested his head on the sofa, and, right then and there, he simply fell apart. It was horrible – he started snivelling, can you imagine, a man like that. I don't even care to remember it. He mumbled something about wanting me to forgive him, he couldn't control himself, it wasn't his fault, it was that filthy cocaine. I'd already figured that one out, my dear, that this man was not in his right mind, desperation like that doesn't come from drinking whiskey. I sat back down and started caressing his head, I told him not to worry, I was his friend, and he could trust me completely; he should go ahead and tell me what was going on, and I would help him get Olga María back. Finally, he calmed down a little. I quickly pulled myself together, straightened out my clothes: I was worried he might call in one of his bodyguards. Then he started telling me the whole story, just like that, still kneeling on the floor, his head resting on my lap, like some kind of naughty child. He told me that with Olga María the same thing had happened, the same despair, the same evil demon ruining everything, because by the time they'd met he was already out of his mind, he'd been snorting cocaine every fifteen minutes, and when Olga María said the same thing I did, that he should take it easy, slow down, he reacted differently, because he'd been wanting her for so long, because he'd been waiting for her for so many years, there was no way he could stop himself, and she, as you can imagine, she tried to get away. Yuca, the idiot, forced her onto the bed. He told me: right there, and pointed to the bedroom where he took her, practically by force, where he ripped off her clothes. She's so strong willed, she rejected him, just like I did. But he didn't stop, like with me; no, he forced himself on top of her and buried his face between her legs, totally possessed, frantic, until Olga María had no choice but to give in, though she was probably disgusted, she must've been. Then it got even

49

worse – that's what tormented Yuca most of all – because of all the drugs he took: he couldn't even get it up. Pathetic, my dear. Can you imagine a hunk of a man like that, right there for the taking, all your very own, and his thingy doesn't even work, all because of his vice!? That's why all that desperation, all that anxiety, wanting to eat and eat and eat, because he knew it didn't work when he was so high on cocaine. A true tragedy. That's when I understood why Olga María had come out so disappointed, why she'd decided not to tell me anything, and why she totally broke off her relationship with Yuca. She did the right thing, my dear, there's no point taking risks with a man like that. But that first time, after his pathetic performance, Yuca told her he was sorry, he begged her to forgive him, he didn't usually act like that or take so many drugs, he promised her it would never happen again, he wouldn't be so high the next time, and that's why Olga María went to him one more time. But the same thing happened: the man was high, impotent, anxious, frantic, all in all pretty pathetic. Like I'm telling you, that's exactly how Yuca told me: he was kneeling on the floor with his head resting on my lap, he was falling apart, sobbing. I know, it's hard to believe. I told him he had only one option: get on the next plane to the States and check himself into a detox clinic. That was the only sensible thing to do, the only way he could save his relationship with Olga María. Yuca took my advice, my dear. I don't know if I was the only one who'd suggested that, but the fact is, three days later, he was on his way to Houston; the official word from the party was that it was for a routine medical exam. Finally, we're moving. I think this is the longest it's ever taken me to get to the cemetery. I told you, after the bridge, the streets are so narrow you can get stuck here for ever; all it takes is one idiot to bring the traffic to a standstill. Of course Olga María and I talked about Yuca. I told her in detail what had happened; well, I didn't tell her I let him kiss me, just in case they started seeing each other again, then I'd be in trouble. When Yuca left for Houston I called to give her the good news, because she wasn't taking his calls. I told her that when Yuca got back and was cured, they could try again. But now you probably understand how Olga María is – she sounded completely offhand when she said she'd never get involved with Yuca again, not for anything in the world, for her that chapter was over and done with, she'd have to be crazy to get involved with a guy like that. Maybe she was right, my dear, but I felt sorry for Yuca, because what motivated him to get treatment was the possibility of seeing Olga María again. That's what I think, anyway – I can't believe he did it for Kati's sake; he's not at all interested in her any more. We're here, my dear. Look how beautiful the lawns are, they're so well manicured. It feels peaceful, doesn't it? This is the best cemetery. They say it belongs to that Arab, Facussé, who also owns Channel 11; apparently he's made a fortune off all the dead people, enough money to buy and run that station. Papa hates him. Well, dear, Papa hates all Arabs, I've never understood why. It's something visceral. He says that before, the Arabs in this country didn't have a pot to piss in, and that it's only thanks to the communists that they now own the country. Papa has his own opinions about these things, and for him, the Arabs are to blame for a whole bunch of bad things. Now that I think about it, he's probably right, because that Deputy Chief Handal must be an Arab. But this cemetery's beautiful, isn't it? Olga María loved it here. Don Sergio is buried here; they'll bury her next to him. It's going to be impossible to park with all these cars here, and it's going to be impossible to get out when it's over. Look at that section over there, I've never seen it before: this cemetery sure has grown, the Arab must be drowning in money. I'm going to park over there, under that tree, next to that arbour, the sun is still pretty strong. Oh, dear, I hope my skirt hasn't got wrinkled. That's what I don't like about this material: it wrinkles too easily. Don't bother: the doors lock automatically. My goodness, what a lot of cars. Come this way. Let's let the family go first. How beautiful they all look next to the coffin: Marito, José Carlos, Yuca and Sergio. The four men who loved her most. I'd even say she'd be happy to see them all together. Let's get closer. Look at Doña Olga, poor thing. What a tragedy, my dear – do you have more Kleenex? The wretches: how could they have done such a thing. They've got no guts. My darling girls, come here.

3. Novena

I'm calling you, my dear, because I didn't manage to tell you about anything during the service. Then my mother started bugging me and I had to go with her to La Galleria to buy a gift to bring to a tea party tomorrow. I couldn't say no. They did a good job on that mall, but I don't like that big old colonial mansion they left right in the middle; they should have torn it down; such a crummy old dump surrounded by all those pretty, modern shops. It took for ever; you know how my mother is when she goes shopping: she can never make up her mind. We got back about fifteen minutes ago. That's why I didn't call you sooner. The service was lovely, wasn't it, my dear? So many people there, and I loved what the priest said about the dead: it fits Olga María to a tee. That thing about pure spirits dedicated to helping others. Beautiful. I like that priest: he only talks about spiritual things; not even a little bit communist, like that Ramírez priest who sometimes says mass at that church. Everybody was there, even José Carlos, who's a committed atheist. Only Papa wasn't there, there's no way to get him to church. I've never seen anybody who hates priests as much as he does – he doesn't care if they're communists, like those Jesuits, or good ones, like that one Olga María got; as far as he's concerned, they're all the same. My mother always feels sad when she arranges to meet her friends at church, and she shows up alone, while they all come with their husbands. Did you see Kati, my dear? She's gained weight. It must be because of her break-up with Yuca. I've heard they're getting a divorce, but that's yet to be seen. I've spoken to Yuca only once since he got back from rehab in Houston. He called me to ask about Olga María. She refused to take his calls, and that's how she left it when she died: once she got an idea in her head, there was no way to make her change her mind. The poor guy returned with a lot of hope that Olga María would get back together with him. He kept at me to convince her that he'd turned over a new leaf – he was a new man, he said. I didn't want him to despair, but I told him it was going to be rough, and he knew how Olga María could be. Then I didn't talk to him again until her funeral, and we barely had a chance to say hi. He was devastated. I'm pretty sure his relationship with Kati has no future, but I don't think they'll divorce. Can you imagine the scandal!? And what Don Federico would say? Yuca has too much to lose. Kati is Don Federico's favourite daughter. I think that's what's driving Yuca crazy, why he got so addicted to cocaine – it's horrible to have to live with someone you can't stand. I should know, I've experienced it in the flesh. Luckily I got rid of Alberto as soon as I could. But poor Yuca, in his political position, with his economic interests, and everything so tied up with Don Federico, he can't just tell Kati to get lost, even though he'd probably like to. I think he already had that figured out and that's why he was pursuing the relationship with Olga María, as a kind of life raft, and it would have been perfect, my dear: to have a mistress you love more than your wife. Though I'm sure Olga María never dreamt of getting involved in anything so serious; of that much I'm certain. But now all that's in the past. But for Kati it must be horrible, too. If I were her, I'd open my heart to Don Federico, make him understand that the marriage simply isn't working out, tell him once and for all that his relationship with Yuca – his economic and political support for Yuca – is one thing, and his daughter's marriage is another thing altogether. But they say that Don Federico is very domineering, very stubborn, so probably Kati's only option is to eat, to calm her nerves, that is. For the same reason Yuca started using cocaine, Kati eats. That's why she's so fat. That's all I can think of, the only thing that makes sense. Don't you agree, my dear? But Kati is no fool, either. Did you see that baggy dress she was wearing? Super-elegant, and it did wonders disguising how fat she's grown. Why lie, we've never got along. She's too full of herself; just because she's got so much more money than somebody else. I also think she knows that Yuca was after my body. What bothers me most about her is that she never stops talking; I swear I've never known anybody who talks as much as Kati. She thinks everybody else needs to listen to all her nonsense. She just won't stop: talk talk talk. I'll admit it: everyone talks more than they should sometimes, it even happens to me once in a while, I get bitten by a talking bug, but I'm small fry compared to her when it comes to non-stop talking. That's why I avoid her, all that endless chattering really grates on my nerves. I don't know how Yuca can stand her; all for Don Federico's money. But what I wanted to tell you is that that Deputy Chief Handal interrogated me for a long time. I couldn't say no. So many things have happened in the last few days since they killed Olga María. Practically the whole country is following the case, especially since they caught the murderer. That's why I agreed to the interrogation, because now that they've already caught the perpetrator, whatever I tell them won't be a waste. It was this morning, Deputy Chief Handal and that bloodhound named Villalta, who's always with him, they came to my house. Papa told me to be careful with these guys, that I should tape the interview myself. Papa said that wasn't a legal interrogation, like part of a trial, it was just an interview. Papa said that if I wanted, he could send over his lawyer to be with me while they were questioning me. But that would make them feel too important and give the impression that despicable people like them are capable of intimidating someone like me. So I preferred to go it alone, with just my tape recorder, in my own living room. I made them wait for about half an hour, just so they wouldn't think we were equals or anything. When I came in, I didn't offer them my hand: people like that can misinterpret even a simple courtesy. I scowled at them and told them to hurry up with their questions, I told them they should thank me for allowing them to interrogate little Olga the afternoon of the murder, and it was thanks to me allowing them to question her that they got the description of the murderer, and if the girl hadn't told them that he looked like Robocop – that cop on television – they'd still be looking for clues. What I wanted to make clear to them was that the credit for capturing Robocop should go to little Olga, not the police. Straight away I asked them about that Robocop person's confession, if they already had the name of the criminal mastermind, I wanted them to tell me more than what the newspapers were saying. But Deputy Chief Handal was super-relaxed, different than I'd seen him before; maybe he's relieved because they've apprehended the murderer. He told me that Robocop still hadn't talked, hadn't confessed to anything, but they were following various lines of investigation that would surely lead them to discover the motives and the mastermind – that's what he said: "the motives and the mastermind". What a clown, he acted like he was on television. I was surprised when first thing he asked me about José Carlos: his friendship with Marito, if he got along with Olga María, why he was making preparations to leave the country. I told him what everybody and his brother knows, though I wasn't going to tell him about José Carlos screwing Olga María. Then he asked me something that left me dumbfounded: if I knew about the existence of some photographs José Carlos took of Olga María stark naked and in obscene positions. I sat there with my mouth hanging open. Olga María never told me about those photos. And that's what I told this Deputy Chief Handal. It's true: I don't know anything about them. That's why I asked him who'd told him such a lie, José Carlos is an artist, I've seen the photos he took of Olga María, and they weren't at all indecent. Then he asked me if I thought José Carlos would be capable of blackmailing the Trabanino family with those photos. Can you imagine how sordid that policeman's mind is!? I got very upset; I told him that first of all those photos don't exist, and second of all, José Carlos was incapable of such a despicable idea – only a rude, shameless policeman like him would think that up. He told me to calm down, he was just trying to disprove certain hypotheses, that was the reason for our interview. I made it very clear to him that I didn't like his style of "investigating", that I had never heard that such slandering of decent, honourable people was called an "investigation" or a "hypothesis". He pretended not to know what I was talking about, instead he asked me if Olga María had been in love with José Carlos or if it was just a short fling. What I can't figure out, my dear, is how this Deputy Chief Handal could have got so much information about that woman's private life. It makes me furious – I would love to know who the big mouth is who goes around making up stories about Olga María. I suspect it's one of two people: Cheli or Conchita. I already warned them they shouldn't go around making things up and talking nonsense, especially to the police, but it looks like they didn't get the message. Did you see them today at the Novena Mass? They looked like innocent little doves. But one of them is a traitor. I'm sure of it. I've gone to the boutique twice to warn them. They tell me not to worry, they wouldn't ruin Doña Olguita's reputation for anything in the world, that's how they still call Olga María. But I know their kind: they can't fool me with that goody-two-shoes act. When I find out who's talking more than they should be, they're going to find out who I am! Shit-heads; I get angry just thinking about it. And then this Deputy Chief Handal takes out a photo of Olga María stretched out on a sofa naked – though without showing her privates. And there's no question José Carlos was the one who took that photo. I swear I couldn't get over the shock. Olga María never told me anything about it. Unbelievable – I thought she trusted me more than that. But it turns out she played her cards close to her chest. Now I don't understand anything. Deputy Chief Handal couldn't contain his delight at seeing me with my mouth hanging open, dumbstruck. Until I asked him where he'd got that photo – he thought I'd already surrendered. But instead of answering my questions he started interrogating me: I shouldn't lie to him, if I knew of the existence of that photo I should just admit it, my cooperation was crucial to the investigation of the murder of my best friend. He emphasized the words "my best friend", in a way I didn't like at all. I managed to pull myself together, rally my strength – I told him he was a thief, he'd probably stolen that picture, he couldn't have got it any other way. He informed me, nonchalantly, that he'd found it among Olga María's belongings. He must have thought I was an imbecile. Can you imagine? How was I supposed to believe that Olga María would keep a photo like that in her house and take the chance of Marito finding it?! Here's what I told him: I didn't believe him, he should take his stories elsewhere, this was clearly doctored, with all these new computer programs anything was possible now, he didn't really believe I was going to fall for his dirty little trick of trying to implicate José Carlos in Olga María's murder. Oh, my dear, poor José Carlos! So deeply in love with Olga María: he would never dream of blackmailing her. I'm sure this Deputy Chief Handal searched José Carlos's studio, found that picture, and wanted to trap me with it. That was his plan. But I had him figured out as soon as he returned to the subject of Yuca: he asked me what I knew about his relationship with Olga María. I just stared at him as if to say, "What a brute!" And that's when he pulled out the ghastly ace he'd been keeping up his sleeve: did I think Madame Berrenechea was upset about the *liaison* between her husband and Madame Trabanino? What a pig! You should have heard how he pronounced the word *liaison*, the brute – I stood up and told him to leave my house immediately, and to be very careful, he was in big trouble if he thought he could go around slandering Kati like that, he clearly had no idea how Don Federico Schultz would react if he found out that some nobody was going around insinuating that his daughter was somehow involved in Olga María's murder. I shouted at him, my dear. Also, that he should be even more careful about Yuca, because I'd already warned Yuca that a policeman in cahoots with the communists was spreading lies about his involvement in Olga María's murder. This is no laughing matter, my dear. The very same day as the burial, the first thing I told Yuca, after taking him a ways away from Kati, was what Deputy Chief Handal was hatching. I could tell this alarmed Yuca – he asked me how that policeman would have found out about his relationship with Olga María. How should I know? But I warned him he should take all the necessary precautions. Yuca is friends with the chief of police, as well as the minister of public safety. I'm surprised they haven't taken this Deputy Chief Handal off the case. I'm telling you all this, my dear, but don't repeat a word of it to anybody; it's all *extremely* delicate. Wait, wait a second, Mama's talking to me. She's telling me to turn on the television, there's a report about the Olga María case on the news. Hold on a minute, it's on Channel 2. I hate watching the news: all they ever do is talk about politics. What a bore. But ever since what happened to Olga María, I've got my ears glued to every word they say. There it is. Are you watching it, too, my dear? Look at that animal: he's really got the mug of a criminal. The more I look at him the more he looks like a murderer to me. They caught him in Soyapango, in a major operation. He's an ex-sergeant from the Acahuapa battalion. They identified him thanks to the girls' description: there aren't many soldiers in this country who look like Robocop. Bastard, creep. Too bad there's no death penalty. They should execute him, like they do in Guatemala – did you see on television the last time they executed an Indian there? They don't stand around there wondering what to do; if you're an Indian and a criminal, you go straight to the firing squad. As it should be. If they've got the death penalty in the most civilized country, the United States, why not here? A guy like that isn't going to suddenly turn into a nice guy. Papa says it's the priests' fault that there's no death penalty – I agree with him: I bet you if they sent a dozen bad guys like him to face the firing squad it might make them think twice before carrying out their atrocities against decent people. Fiends like that don't respond to reason. With that criminal look in his eyes, you think he could be reformed? They should shoot him, without a trial or anything. Well, of course, first he should give the name of the mastermind, even though a brute like that never squeals. But I didn't finish telling you about this Deputy Chief Handal's visit. I thought he was going to take off right away after my screaming fit, but he didn't even stand up. The one who was terrified, like he wanted to hide under the sofa, like a mongrel who was being beaten, was the detective who came with him, that Villalta person – just looking at him you'd think he was that bastard Robocop's brother. What kind of a world is this? As I was saying, this Deputy Chief Handal remained very calm, sitting there in that armchair, staring at me, like I was whispering sweet nothings in his ear. Then he said that if I'd got everything off my chest, I might like to sit down again, he wanted to finish up so he wouldn't have to bother me again. He said it so gently it caught me off guard. I actually listened. He went back to the subject of Yuca, and Kati, and Olga María. He assured me he had no intention of judging anybody's private life, much less a person who'd been murdered in such a brutal way, but his job consisted of pursuing all possible lines of investigation, and one of them was pointing to a crime of passion, though this wasn't the only or even the most important one. He told me he had specific information about Olga María's relationship with José Carlos and with Yuca, and he understood, I'd prefer not to talk about those things, I'd fiercely defend my friend's private life, but the information he had led him to believe that I was aware of these relationships. This Deputy Chief Handal spoke so gently, without any hostility, that I couldn't get upset, my dear. All I managed to do was ask where he'd got his information. He told me he couldn't reveal his sources, in his line of work he had to maintain strict confidentiality – anything I told him he would keep in the strictest secrecy, I should trust him. His goal in questioning me was only to dig a little deeper into the relationships Olga María had with her friends, not to create a scandal or anything like that, just to tie up the loose ends of that line of investigation. That's what he said, then he added that his work was apolitical, that he never had any intention of messing with Don Gastón Berrenechea's reputation, much less that of his wife. And maybe because I'm so tired of all this, maybe because his tone of voice was so gentle, maybe because, when all is said and done, the man is doing his job because he did arrest the murderer, well, the truth is I began to answer most of his questions. I told him, yes, José Carlos was in love with Olga María, they'd met on several occasions, in his studio, and Marito didn't know anything about it. But I made it clear to him that I didn't know anything about any pornographic pictures or any blackmail, the truth was I considered José Carlos incapable of doing anything of the sort. Then I told him in no uncertain terms that if he wanted me to keep talking he'd have to tell me where he'd got that photograph of Olga María. He repeated that he couldn't tell me. I asked him if there were other photos or if this was the only one. Since he kept quiet, my dear, I kept my mouth shut. I told them the interview was over, to please leave because I felt very tired. Here comes my mother. Wait a second. She says the Brazilian telenovela is about to start. Yes, we watch it together, hard as that is to believe. I know, I also never imagined my mother would like a telenovela like that – it's so racy, so sexy. But she's taken even more of a liking to it than me: she hasn't missed a single episode. I love it. In a totally different league than that Mexican garbage, only servants watch that. But it bugs me that it's so long, it seems like it'll never end; the one I like best is that Holofernes – what a hunk, my dear, incredible man, gorgeous, but with such a horrible name; I wonder what his name is in real life. If it weren't for Holofernes I'd have stopped watching that telenovela. The truth is there's ten more minutes before it starts; my mother's always jumping the gun. Anyway, I pretended to be tired, I didn't want to talk any more, but this Deputy Chief Handal was determined to finish the job, because he didn't budge, he asked me if Olga María's relationships with José Carlos and Yuca had overlapped, which had come first, if either one knew of the existence of the other, if Marito suspected or knew anything. I told him more or less what we know, but without going into many details, because, when all's said and done, the guy already had the information, it didn't do anybody any good for me to play the fool. What I did do was let him know that only a total imbecile would ever suspect someone as important as Gastón Berrenechea, with his political and economic interests, of hiring someone to kill the woman he loved, which would only create thousands of problems for himself. That's what I told him: Yuca would be the last person with any interest in Olga María being dead, he could be sure of that. Then he asked me about Kati. But the truth is I don't know if she realized what was going on between Olga María and her husband, and I don't think she'd care, anyway. Why would you care if the husband you can't stand any more goes out with one woman or another? Why would she even bother to ask, my dear? That's what happened to me. The thing is, Alberto is so boring I don't think he could even get a woman to go out with him unless he first shows her his bank account. That's why I told this Deputy Chief Handal, this line of investigation that points to a "crime of passion", as he calls it, doesn't make much sense: neither José Carlos nor Yuca nor Kati, much less Marito, would have anything to gain from Olga María's death. That was my conclusion, my dear, though afterwards I started wondering how anyone can ever be sure of what anybody else thinks or feels. Just look at Olga María: not to have shown me, not to have even mentioned the naked photo José Carlos took of her! And Yuca, during one of his panic attacks, mortified by jealousy and a woman's abject scorn, with all that power at his disposal, what wouldn't he be capable of? That interview with the police has affected me strongly, believe it or not. I've started imagining horrible things about Kati, God help me, all because of that policeman's filthy insinuations; for instance, maybe she found out about Yuca and Olga María's *affaire* and she arranged the murder to create problems for Yuca. Pure fantasy, of course, as if I'd been force-fed a bunch of murder mysteries, but that's how that interview with this Deputy Chief Handal affected me. Can you believe that it never occurred to me that Don Federico himself could have masterminded Olga María's murder and that way kill three birds with one stone: finish off the woman who was driving his son-in-law crazy, save his daughter's marriage, and keep Yuca on a tighter leash because of the suspicions that would surround him. Yes, I know, my dear, more fantasy – things like that only happen in telenovelas. It's that meddlesome, conniving policeman, he's to blame for what's happening to me, but before he left I asked him what his other lines of investigation were, other than the "crime of passion" one, just in case I could contribute anything to them. The guy didn't want to give me even a little hint; he just told me that if he uncovers anything of interest or if he needs to talk to me again, he'd call me. That's what he called it: "talk to me", as if it weren't really an interrogation. He gave me a little card so I'd get in touch with him if I remembered anything important that would help the investigation. In short, he came here to mess with my head. That was this morning; they were at the house until noon. It was their fault I was upset all afternoon. You see, I've even started thinking badly of Marito, God forbid, as if the poor man didn't have enough sorrows and problems. The mind can be a treacherous thing: you know, I even started wondering if maybe Marito had a lover, if he found out about the *affaire* between Yuca and Olga María and saw his chance to get rid of her *and* point the finger at Yuca *and* get the insurance money. Yes, my dear, I know, it's despicable. I feel guilty just thinking such thoughts. It's all this Deputy Chief Handal's fault. That's why I went to see the girls after lunch, to Doña Olga's place, because the situation is so chaotic, the girls spend most of the time at their grandmother's, but Marito wants to be with them at least for meals. The horrible thing is that the house reminds them of Olga María's murder. Can you imagine how awful it must be for the girls to walk into that living room where that monster murdered their mother? It can't be good for them. I already told Marito: he should sell that house immediately. If he doesn't, the girls will never get over their trauma. They should live in a different house, a different space, where they can forget that atrocity – Marito agrees with me. But it's not so easy to sell the house and buy another one. It'll take a few months. In the meantime it's best for the girls to live at Doña Olga's and go home only to get their clothes and toys – the less they go there the better. The one who has it the worst is Julita: she can't go to Doña Olga's – her place is too small and also they can't leave

Olga María's house with nobody there, with so many thieves around who'd strip it bare in the blink of an eye. The poor thing has been totally abandoned, because Marito comes home only to sleep. Poor dear Julita, I really feel sorry for her, all alone in that house, full of so many memories, with Olga María's presence everywhere, with nothing much to do, not being able to see the girls, like living with ghosts. It's horrible. Doña Olga agrees with me. We talked about it this afternoon, when I went to see the girls. Something has to be done about Julita, she's worked for them for so many years. But for now there's nothing to do: neither Sergio nor Cuca nor Doña Olga can take her to live with them. She'll have to wait until Marito moves, the girls get settled again, and then Julita can take care of them. In the meantime that poor woman might go crazy; that's what I'm worried about. Here comes my mother, again. Wait a second. She says the Brazilian telenovela has started. I'm going to have to go, or else my mother won't be able to enjoy it. I'll call you later, or tomorrow morning if you're going out tonight. It's just that I have a few more ideas about this Deputy Chief Handal's suspicions, a couple of ideas that might help find the mastermind behind Olga María's murder. I want to explain them to you – but not in such a rush – so you can give me your opinion. I'm even tempted to call that policeman so he can follow up on some leads. But they're very delicate issues. Let's talk about it later. OK, ciao.

4. The Balcony

I love this place, my dear; it's the second time I've been here. About a month ago we sat at this very table with Olga María. What I like is its European *ambiance*, how you don't feel like you're in San Salvador – the only thing missing is air conditioning to make it perfect. I prefer this side, facing the street, each table with its own little balcony. I still have my doubts about this neighbourhood; I wish it were in one of the better residential neighbourhoods, but it's not that bad here. Look at all the traffic. That mall across the street, it's done in such poor taste, it's so tacky, more for servants than anybody else. Did you know Mirna Leiva owns this place, that classmate of ours from the American School? I don't see her here now. Last time she was tending bar. She lived abroad for several years, after her major difficulties. Remember they arrested her for being a communist? Poor thing. She spent several years in Madrid. Her grandparents are from there. At one time the three of us were close friends, yes, with Olga María, we were about thirteen, I think it was before high school, but later we grew apart, especially after they arrested her and there was that big scandal. I don't understand how she could have got mixed up with the communists. She comes from a good family, they've got coffee plantations. Poor woman, they dis-inherited her, things turned out badly for her. But now with this place she's doing super-well. A real success story. It's worth every penny: the wine and food are very reasonable, considering the quality. We came at night with Olga María. We ordered a bottle of French white wine and a plate of cheese and cold cuts. Everything was delicious. We talked and talked. I think that was the last time we talked so much with her. She looked gorgeous that night, with her black miniskirt and high-heeled boots. Stunning; I never saw her looking so sexy. First, we checked the whole place out; around the other side, behind the bar, they have foreign magazines and newspapers, in case you come alone and want to read. Then we picked this table. Olga María was kind of sad – it was her disappointment with Yuca and her problems with Marito – but after a few glasses of wine she got livelier, happy, she started having a good time. Check it out: the best thing about this place are the waiters, all university students, handsome devils, every one, to drool over. They say Mirna picks the gorgeous ones on purpose, so women get addicted to coming here. Evil tongues, my dear; even though, if I were Mirna, who knows if I'd resist the temptation to give a few of them a whirl. That one over there is the one who waited on us when we came with her. Gorgeous, isn't he? I think his name is Rodolfo. You should have seen Olga María that night! She didn't stop chatting up that Rodolfo. Every time he walked by she called him over and started plying him with questions. She was making the poor thing very nervous. Olga María could be quite a handful when she got tipsy. The kid told us he was in his second year at medical school, he told us almost all the waiters were at the university, and he didn't have a girlfriend. But he's not going to wait on us, look, it'll be this one. He's not bad, either. What do you want to drink? It's only five thirty. Too early for wine. I'd like a cappuccino and an apple tart. And bring me a glass of water, you hear? What did I tell you? Though he seems kind of stupid. Look over there, in the red car, isn't that Cuca? It's her. Of course, it is. What's she doing in this part of town? Poor thing, that Cuca, she just doesn't measure up to Sergio. I don't understand how such an attractive man ended up in that woman's hands, even though, it's true, she is a nice person. Anyway, that night, with Olga María, you should have seen how much fun we had. In the end, we got a bit outrageous, but we kept our voices down, whispering, so nobody would hear us. She kept saying she wanted to take that dreamboat home with us, she wanted to eat him up. Yes, my dear, after a few glasses of wine everything gets topsy-turvy. She asked me if I'd be willing for the two of us to go to bed with the same man. We were a little off our rockers by then. Olga María surprised me: she was always so reserved, so proper, so low-key, so modest. But that night she was like a different woman, magically transformed, as if the wine had revealed her hidden self, I don't know, my dear, but she was happy, free, after a while she didn't mention her relationship with Marito, or the girls, or the business, she was just fantasizing about what we'd do with that cute waiter I just showed you, how we'd handle him between the two of us. Later, I thought maybe her failure with Yuca, her disappointment, might have affected her mood.

She even asked me certain questions you don't go around asking any day of the week. For example, she wanted to know what my biggest sexual fantasy was, my ultimate sexual fantasy, what I imagined would feel the absolute best and what would be very difficult, if not impossible, to do. Yes, I'm not lying to you, at this very table. I think that waiter unleashed her desires, or who knows what. Here he comes with the cappuccinos. This kid is good-looking but he doesn't set loose in you what got set loose in Olga María that night. Not even close. That was the last time I saw her so happy, as if she already had some premonition of her own death and wanted to enjoy life to the fullest. She told me that her sexual fantasy, what she would like to try before she died – how incredible, my dear, I still remember those very words: "what I would like to try before I die" – was to be in bed with two men at the same time. I think we all have that fantasy. Don't you? I asked her which two, because it's not the same to go to bed with two ugly idiots as with two hunks you have the hots for. There's so much traffic. This time of day is always crazy. Look at that jam. That's what's so stressful: too many cars. I hope it clears up by the time we leave. What do you think she answered? That at that moment the only one she could think of was that waiter, Rodolfo, I said his name was. Poor Olga María. When you think about it, it must be awful to live with the same man for almost ten years, even if you do love him and have kids with him. Can you imagine always screwing the same way, because no matter what, you always get into some kind of routine.

That's what happened to me with Alberto, and we lived together for barely a year. Horrible. But Alberto is a special case. I don't know how I ever got together with that man. Thank God I freed myself from his clutches. He doesn't have a shred of imagination. I was always the one who had to get on top of him: he never took the initiative. I think that man could live perfectly well without sex. I like being on top, but not all the time. I'm telling you, I was always the one who had to be in charge: he just lay there in bed, with his undershirt and shorts on, like a plank of wood. Of course: he claimed that he'd catch cold if he took off his underpants and T-shirt. What a calamity. I don't know if all financiers are such prudes – and I don't want to find out. This cappuccino is delicious, isn't it? You can tell it's a real cappuccino; in most places they just whip up the milk a little and pour it into any old coffee and call it a cappuccino; what a fiasco. Taste the cake, dear: it's divine. Let me ask this kid if they make it here. No, right? That's what I thought. That time with Olga María we didn't try the cakes; just wine and cheese and cold cuts. As I was saying, she was in this super-liberated mood, and she told me that at the very beginning of her relationship with Marito she told him about her fantasy of sleeping with two men, but instead of going along with her, he got angry. Men are such brutes. Don't go getting any ideas that Marito is some kind of saint. He's nowhere near as bad as Alberto, needless to say, but it's just that men, once they've got you, they don't worry about it any more. Olga María told me she was sick of Marito, in bed

I mean, that he always went through the same ritual: he rubbed cream on his hands and started massaging her legs, then her hips, until his thing stood up, and then he got on top of her. Always the same. When she told me, I told her she shouldn't complain, a man massaging your legs before making love is nothing to sneer at. I told her again about my experience with Alberto. Nobody's ever done it to me that way, starting out with a leg massage. But she told me she hated the cream, she didn't want anything more to do with a man who massaged her legs with cream before fucking her. Now I understand her: ten years of having the same thing done to you is enough to drive you crazy. That's why she had such a good time with Julio Iglesias and José Carlos; she'd put up with being only with Marito for a long time. Now that I think about it, that must have been her disappointment with Yuca: just imagine, you've been waiting for this man to ravish you, and to do it with the full force of his virility and his imagination, and it turns out the man's so strung out, he can't even get it up. It could even make you feel resentful. Speaking of Yuca, here's what I wanted to tell you: I think some political enemy of Yuca's might have hired somebody to murder Olga María, in order to hurt him, to implicate him in a crime, you know, like the "crime of passion" hypothesis Deputy Chief Handal is considering. Doesn't that sound logical to you? I've been thinking about it. That's the only way it makes sense that someone actually plotted and planned such an atrocity. Did you hear, that monster who shot her was a soldier, one of those specially trained ones in the Acahuapa battalion. Any one of those unscrupulous military people might have arranged the murder. Yes, my dear, a whole slew of officers want to get into politics, seeing as how the war is over and they can't keep stealing like they used to – they've got to adapt to the changing circumstances. This is all very hush-hush. At first I considered mentioning it to Deputy Chief Handal, but what if he's in cahoots with the mastermind and that's why he's trying to steer the investigation toward a "crime of passion" – so he can smear Yuca and poor Olga María? It makes me furious. But it wouldn't be the first time they've tried to slander Yuca with this kind of thing. Now that I think about it, when they arrested Mirna for being a communist, people went around saying the whole thing was Yuca's fault, he'd turned her in because she refused to sleep with him, and Mirna was actually innocent and it was just his way of taking revenge. I never believed a word of it. Nothing but idle gossip. Yuca didn't need to do something like that to Mirna. But Olga María didn't agree with me: she said that during that period Yuca was obsessed with hunting down communists, he was pretty messed up, and it wouldn't have been unheard of for him to destroy Mirna's life out of pure spite. Because they did destroy her life, my dear. Poor Mirna disappeared for three days, and it was only because her family pulled strings in high places that they sent her to the women's prison. But while she was missing with the National Guard, they raped her. That's what they say, anyway. Who knows how many. Horrible. Just thinking about it gives me the shivers: can you imagine a whole bunch of disgusting drooling torturers, one after the other climbing on top of you, sticking that putrid thing, full of diseases, in you? I'd vomit; I'd die. Poor Mirna. When she was released, they sent her to Madrid. Seems like now she stays out of trouble, but she still has a reputation for being a bit of a red and a little off her rocker. Papa says they don't arrest anybody for no reason, Mirna must have been involved in something. I agree: Yuca had nothing to do with it. You want to order something else? I feel like a glass of wine. There's still a lot of traffic. I don't want to drink more coffee: I won't be able to sleep. I'd prefer white wine. Do you see the pictures? The paintings on the walls, dear. They give this place a special *cachet*, something *artistique*. Even though I don't know anything about art – here comes the waiter. Are you going to drink the other cappuccino? That idea that Yuca's political enemies could have masterminded Olga María's murder, I mentioned it to José Carlos. Yesterday at noon. We had lunch together. Didn't I tell you? It was lovely. We went to Marea Alta Restaurant in the Zona Rosa. No, I called to ask him where that Deputy Chief Handal had got that photo of Olga María. No, I didn't just come out and ask him like that, so abruptly, I said we should talk, the police had been interrogating me and I'd like to talk to him about it. José Carlos has already packed up his studio, and he's leaving for Boston next Monday. He invited me out for lunch. He's so sweet. He said that way we could say a proper goodbye, because he'll be running around like crazy all weekend, here and there, tying up loose ends, because he's decided to leave for good – he doesn't plan to live in this country ever again. He's very upset, my dear. How could he not be? You should have heard some of the things he told me. He's taken it hard, poor man. That's why he invited me out to eat at Marea Alta, because he doesn't have a studio or anything. Too bad, my dear, I would have rather gone to his studio. But we had a great time. We drank beer and ate oysters. Upstairs. I love that place: you're up there level with the treetops, hidden, you can see the cars going by but they can't see you. I wanted to know what José Carlos had talked about with this Deputy Chief Handal, what muddled drivel that scandal-mongering policeman came to him with – here comes the waiter with my wine. It's delicious, ice cold. Excuse me, young man, that other waiter's name is Rodolfo, isn't it? Yes, that one behind the bar. What did I tell you? When he walks by I'm going to tell him about Olga María. He probably hasn't heard. Of course he'll remember her. How could he forget? Are you nuts? A woman like Olga María isn't easy to forget, especially when she's been flirting with you; there's not a man in the world who'd forget that. I'm going to call him over here. No, it's not tactless. Anyway, I want to finish telling you about José Carlos. The thing is, I asked him point blank where this Deputy Chief Handal had got the naked photograph of Olga María – though it doesn't show her privates – lying on the sofa; I told him I knew that he, José Carlos, had taken that picture, he shouldn't try to pull the wool over my eyes, I knew that sofa and it would have been very unlikely that a brute like Handal would be going around fabricating a photo like that – he should be frank with me. He was surprised that the policeman would have been so indiscreet as to show me the picture of Olga María. Needless to say, he did take the picture: it was one in a series he thought up one afternoon when she came to the studio and they were drinking wine. They were already pretty tipsy, and José Carlos suggested she pose in the nude, but only in suggestive poses, without showing her privates: neither her tits nor her pussy. He told me he shot a whole roll, but that night Olga María called him, very alarmed, and asked him to destroy the roll – she said taking those photos had been totally reckless. That's what José Carlos told me, anyway. He told her he'd already developed them, in his own darkroom, and the pictures had come out fantastic, he wanted to show them to her. But Olga María was really worried: she begged him to destroy the prints and the negatives, said she'd pay him for the cost of the materials, she just didn't want those photos to exist for anything in the world. The whole thing had been madness, she'd never allow him to take pictures of her again. José Carlos said he'd never heard her so beside herself, so categorical, and he promised her he'd destroy them all. And that's what he did. But he kept one, the brute, and he left it in his album as a souvenir. According to him, Deputy Chief Handal and his blood-hounds searched his entire studio, without permission or a warrant, and they illegally confiscated the photograph

– the only thing they took, but he can't report them because then Marito would find out about his relationship with Olga María. A great big mess, my dear. Those policemen are a bunch of delinquents. José Carlos says they were very threatening when they interrogated him – he thought any minute they'd arrest him and start torturing him. Horrible: they accused him of blackmailing Olga María and then hiring somebody to murder her when she threatened to report him. Imagine that. Poor José Carlos, he's devastated. But we had a great time upstairs at the Marea Alta, they have these gigantic oysters, absolutely delicious. What José Carlos also doesn't understand is how the police found out about the relationship between him and Olga María. I told him I suspect Conchita and Cheli, the girls from the boutique. But he doesn't want to know anything about it, he just wants to get out of here and never come back. Anybody in his situation would do exactly the same thing. What freaked him out most was that Olga María had had a relationship with Yuca. Deputy Chief Handal, the damn blabbermouth, told him. José Carlos thinks she left him so she could get involved with Yuca: he feels hurt, betrayed, over such a minor thing, but then he really loved her, my dear. I tried to explain to him that Olga María didn't leave him because of Yuca, they'd known each other since their school days, and the whole rest of the story. But he didn't believe me. He looked so upset I couldn't help telling him that Olga María and Yuca never actually made love, I had it from the horse's mouth, he should believe me, things between them never worked out. This all happened yesterday: I played the role of the counsellor, the mender of broken hearts. José Carlos is so sensitive – at one point he even had tears in his eyes, real tears. I told him that Olga María loved him, she'd always spoken highly of him, she'd even confided in me that he was an excellent lover. That's the only way I could comfort him, my dear, men and their vanity. That was when I asked him what he thought about my idea that maybe one of Yuca's friends had arranged for Olga María to be murdered in order to destroy Yuca politically. He mulled it over for a few minutes. Then he said that if that's what happened we'd never find anything out, these kinds of dirty tricks between politicos never come out in the open – Yuca himself would make sure the facts were never known. You sure you don't want a glass of wine? He told me something else that makes sense to me now that I think about it: if one of Yuca's political enemies is responsible for Olga María's murder, it's better that we don't know and don't try to find out who it was, because if we do, they'll kill us, too – and he, in that case, should disappear as soon as possible, because those politicos will try to divert public attention, and there's no better way to do that than have as a scapegoat some photographer nobody would stand up for. José Carlos was getting more and more upset. But I told him not to worry, nobody's going to think he had anything to do with this, even this Deputy Chief Handal doesn't really suspect José Carlos. That's my impression, anyway, my dear. That's what I told him, I was trying to get him to calm down upstairs at Marea

Alta, with those gigantic oysters – so delicious, they made
you want to go straight to the beach. And that's when I
got the idea. I asked José Carlos what he was doing that
afternoon. He said nothing important: just finish packing
a few things, make a few phone calls to say goodbye. I
suggested we go to the beach, to my family's place. He
stared at me like I must be joking. But I wasn't joking: I
suddenly felt like going to the beach, feeling the cool
breeze, stopping thinking about this whole mess with
Olga María. Here's how I explained it to him: it would do
him good to go to the beach, forget for a while all the
horrors we've been through, nothing like the peace and
serenity of the sea to help you relax and bid farewell to
this country. It didn't take much to convince him. We paid
and went straight to the beach, in my car, happy as clams.
You can't imagine what a good time we had. But let me
order another glass of wine. Shall I order one for you? Or
better yet, my dear, let's order a bottle, OK? You're right,
it's too early: a half-bottle, then. Look how this place is
filling up. It's definitely the *in* place. Lots of foreigners.
Every night it's bursting at the seams. In this city it's not
easy to find places like this – José Carlos likes it: he told
me he's been here several times and he's even given Mirna
some tips about how to display the paintings and artistic
photographs. Of course they know each other, my dear;
I've even heard that Mirna was doing it with him. I asked
José Carlos, but he told me they were just friends, Mirna's
not his type, ever since being with Olga María he hasn't
been able to get interested in anybody else. Go figure. But

yesterday afternoon when we went to the beach we made a pact: we'd avoid talking about Olga María so we wouldn't get depressed, so we could enjoy the trip. We went to San Blas. Of course, my dear, I prefer our place in La Barra de Santiago, but it's too far away. The idea was to go for a little while, a few hours in the afternoon. We bought some beer at the port. Poor José Carlos: we didn't mention Olga María, but he spent the whole time talking about Marito. Please, do me a favour! He's full of guilt, remorse, I can't tell you how much. And really afraid, terrified: what scares him most is that Marito will find out about his *affaire* with Olga María. He kept asking me over and over if I think Marito has already found out. I have no idea. That's what I told him. The only one who could let the cat out of the bag is this Deputy Chief Handal, if he goes blabbing to Marito. José Carlos says he's afraid of the same thing: of that policeman showing Marito the photo of Olga María. That's why he wants to leave the country as soon as possible, and avoid the whole thing: it would be degrading, unbearable. Marito has been one of his best friends, if not his very best. But that's how men are, my dear, who told him to get involved with his best friend's wife? Now there's only sorrow. He told me about his friendship with Marito: how they lived in the same neighbourhood, went to the same school, were in the same grade, even the same class. Can you imagine? They spent their entire lives together. Olga María already told me the whole story. That's why when we got to San Blas I told him that talking about Marito was another way of talking about Olga María, so he was violating our pact. I told him it'd be better if he told me about his plans, what he was going to do in Boston. He's really lovely, José Carlos. Now I understand why Olga María fell for him. He's sensitive. His way of seeing the world, even though it's different from yours or mine, is very interesting, he's an artist, after all. He told me he's not sure he has a job in Boston, but he's not worried about it, he lived there long enough to find something that'll let him get by. What he doesn't want to do is work in advertising any more; he finds that environment unbearable – he told me he's planning to work on a major exhibition of his photographs, pick the best ones, and go for it, try to get into the major leagues. That's what he said, like he was talking about baseball: "the major leagues". Shall I pour you more wine? Jesus Christ: look at how those people are dressed. God save me. And that frightful-looking creature, where did she come from? Look at that one with the miniskirt: she looks like she's a cellulite saleswoman. People no longer have any sense of the ridiculous, my dear; vulgar is as vulgar does. The beach was lovely, empty, and it was low tide, that's the good thing about going during the week: the lower classes can't get there. On weekends it's unbearable: all that riff-raff from El Majahual, they simply invade San Blas. They're all thieves and whores. I don't understand why they can't just fence it off – that's what Papa says. If you have a place at the beach you have to put up with all those scum who come there just looking for someone to mug. Horrible. The

beaches should be gated to prevent all that El Majahual
garbage from invading San Blas. But Papa says you can't
do that, legally; I say, to hell with the law. But during the
week it's peaceful, like yesterday afternoon with José
Carlos, we had a wonderful time at the beach. Though he
didn't go in the water – he was stubborn, he didn't want
to wear one of my father's swimsuits; I have some bikinis
there so I took a dip, I went out to the breakwater, it felt
so good being tossed about by the waves. Then we sat
under the almond trees, next to the swimming pool, just
talking. I don't know if I should tell you this, my dear, but
now I understand why Olga María had such a thing for
José Carlos, even if he does dress like a scruffy slob. He's
got a charm all his own, like you wouldn't believe. But let
me ask for a glass of water, this wine has made me thirsty.
Here he comes. Do you want some, too? I can't seem to
get Rodolfo's attention so he'll come over here, the cutie
pie. As I was saying, we were next to the pool when the
couple who looks after the house said they were going to
the port to do some shopping. I told them to go right
ahead, no problem, we were just staying a few hours, we
weren't going to spend the night. You remember the house
in San Blas, don't you? It's very secure because of the big
wall all around it. You can't see the sea from inside, but
nobody can see in from the outside. Like Papa says: it
protects against thieves and peeping Toms. Thank you,
waiter. I was dying of thirst. Let's finish the bottle. We
were alone, José Carlos and I, next to the pool. Then I
said I was going to take a dip, and I'd take advantage of

nobody being around to swim naked. There's nothing better than swimming naked: you feel free. I love it so much that every chance I get, I swim naked. Maybe because I'd already had a few beers or because I already felt comfortable around José Carlos or because the surroundings were so pleasant, whatever it was I wasn't feeling shy. I dived in and once I was in the water I took off my bikini, placed it on the edge of the pool, and started to swim, happy as can be, as if the rest of the world didn't exist. That's what I was doing, swimming on my back, blinded by the sunlight, totally enjoying myself, when I felt José Carlos next to me. Can you imagine, my dear? Like getting an electric shock. Everything happened very quickly. It was amazing. You've never done it in a swimming pool? Unbelievable. That man is a bombshell. He gave it to me every which way. Delicious. His equipment: it's off the charts, enough to make you drool. We did it in the pool, on the grass under the almond trees, in the hammock, in the chaise longue, all over the house. Just remembering it makes me wet again. That José Carlos, he's a darling. He left me utterly exhausted, aching – he does it with imagination. You should really give him a whirl before he leaves. An expert. Now I know why Olga María didn't want to tell me too many details, so I wouldn't get any ideas about him. I don't understand how she let him go. Having a lover like that is worth the trouble, even if he does fall in love with you, who cares, you just deal with it. Of course, it's easy for me to say because I know he's leaving the country, so he doesn't have a chance to fall in love with me. But to marry him and live with him? No, thank you, my dear, God forbid. And definitely not someone to leave your husband for, who you already have a child with, like Olga María with Marito. He's a nobody. This photography thing is fine as a hobby, but nobody respectable can make a living off it. I can just imagine Papa if I said I was going to marry a poor photographer; he'd think I'd gone crazy. He'd disown me. No, he's only for a fling. Well, my dear, when we finished – lying in the hammock, my pussy red and swollen from so much in and out – I asked him if he'd done it like that with Olga María, if he'd lasted that long with her. Because the man can last with his thing standing at attention for an eternity, it's really something, and you get to do whatever you feel like. He told me that with her it had also been special, even the first time, but Olga María was more reserved, more restrained, with me he felt more free. That's what he told me, anyway. Also that he liked my body better than Olga María's, because I'm more curvaceous, fuller, compared to her. I don't know. He told me he thinks my body is voluptuous and Olga María's is more delicate. He prefers voluptuousness. That's another charming thing about José Carlos: he explains things so well. I love the way he talks, the words he chooses, you can clearly understand what he wants to say. The weirdest thing is that we'd made a pact not to talk about Olga María, and there we were, naked and in each other's arms in the hammock, sweaty, exhausted and thinking about her. At a certain point, I got sad. I felt like crying because life is shit, how could it be that Olga María had disappeared from one moment to the next. I mentioned that to José Carlos, then I got tears in my eyes. He was so tender to me, and he got sad, too, then he started comforting me, telling me there's no way to fight fate, Olga María wouldn't have wanted us to be sad. Then I started sobbing, because there's no good reason for so much injustice. José Carlos started caressing me, stroking my head, whispering sweet nothings in my ear, until I calmed down and we started kissing again. That man can turn me on in the blink of an eye, my dear. A moment later, we were at it again, hard and fast, there in the hammock, but more intensely, as if remembering Olga María had injected us with renewed passion, something delicious, something I've never felt before. I swear: it was spectacular. Like I was possessed. Then I started to come in this incredible way, while I was still crying. That's where we were, right at the climax, when the caretakers opened the door. It was horrible, my dear, because I couldn't disengage, I couldn't stop: my feet were on the ground, and I was on top of that man in the hammock, at the peak of my frenzy, knowing the caretakers were about to walk in. I can't even talk about it, it was such a horrible experience. And I only just managed to shout, "Don't come in!" That was when José Carlos realized what was happening. We dashed into the bedroom where I'd left my clothes. So embarrassing. The worst part was that we couldn't finish like we should have. Let's order another half-bottle, my dear. I'm already tipsy. Look, here comes Rodolfo, that doll. I'm going to tell him about Olga María. Rodolfo!

5. Thirty Days

I'm so glad we sat here in the back, my dear, in the last row, so we can chat, even if only in a whisper, quietly. There's been so much going on. Anyway, I don't want to see that priest up close. Papa's right: all priests are twisted and corrupt, but this one has turned out to be a real scoundrel. Did you hear what he did to poor Yuca? It's all anybody's talking about. Yuca's become the laughing stock of the entire world. It's all a plot. They say it's his political enemies. The press has turned against him, too. Luckily they haven't mentioned anything about Olga María. I told you they were going to use the Olga María thing to try to finish Yuca off, and that's exactly what's happened, even if they don't say so publicly, they've started accusing him of other things. They already made him resign from the leadership of the party. Terrible. The man who is far and away the best leader, and the most charismatic – everybody was supporting him. They've done him in – just because of that car they say he stole. A Mercedes Benz this damned priest sold him and now says he doesn't know anything about. No, my dear, I haven't been able to talk to Yuca. He's been too busy: he's at the very centre of a political storm – fending off the low blows, defending his reputation. What worries me is that he'll get hooked on coke again, he'll sink back into a cycle of depression and turn to drugs. They haven't stopped attacking him – just look at the media. How possible is it: a high-ranking leader of the government party buying a stolen car!? What idiots! But the way they say it, it makes people think he's somehow involved in the stolen-car racket, as if Yuca needed to be, like he isn't rich enough already. They set a trap for him, and that no-good priest helped lure him into it. I'm sure of it! Yes, my dear, I'll lower my voice, it's just that I get so furious when I realize what they're doing to that man. They've ruined his political career, and now they want to sink him completely. It's not fair. But that's not the worst of it; the worst is what people are saying in private, what people everywhere are mumbling about under their breath. Horrible: people you thought were Yuca's friends are now out to slander him, they're saying awful things, like he ordered Olga María's murder because she was threatening to expose him as a drug trafficker. Can you imagine? It makes me furious. It's one thing that the man's an addict and another that he's involved in drug trafficking. People say such vile things. Even to me, and they know I'm his friend, you wouldn't believe the atrocious things they insinuate; that happened a few days ago – at the Club no less. According to this person, the gringos discovered Yuca's connection with the drug traffickers, and they decided to take him out of the running, politically speaking, but since they couldn't expose him without spreading the shit all over other high-ranking government officials, they decided to invent this whole farce about the stolen car. Nobody in his right mind can actually believe something like that.

Others are saying that Yuca, in a fit of cocaine-induced madness, hired someone to kill Olga María, and the authorities found out, and when he refused to resign, they invented this scandal about the stolen car. What a mess. All fantasies. Yuca never would have had Olga María killed. I'm not denying that he gets crazy sometimes, but it would never have occurred to him to hurt that woman. All I know for sure is that Yuca insists he bought that Mercedes from this priest. So it must be true. But now the priest is playing the fool and says he knows nothing about the car. Just look at him, that hypocrite up there saying mass, as if nothing were wrong. Poor Olga María, if she knew that despicable priest, who is part of a plot to destroy Yuca, is the one saying her requiem mass, she'd die of outrage – I'm sure of it. It would make her furious. I had no idea he'd be the priest. If I'd known, I'd have warned Doña Olga. I just realized it, just now when I walked into the church – that's why I stayed here in the back row, as a form of protest. That's what I explained to Mama when she asked me why I was sitting way back here: nothing in the world would get me to sit in the front row and listen to that scheming priest. I'm so glad you came, too. I swear, the only reason I'm staying at all is to show my respect for Olga María. On the way out I'm going to ask Doña Olga why she chose that priest. But she's been pretty out to lunch ever since the murder; she's completely devoted to those girls. Maybe it wasn't even her who chose that disgusting priest; it could have been Cuca or Sergio, or even Marito himself. Something's not right, now that I'm thinking about it. Don't you think maybe they chose this priest so that Yuca wouldn't show up? I'm not crazy, or paranoid. With everything that's going on, you imagine the worst. Picking this priest was the best way to stop Yuca from coming. Seeing as how people always think the worst of other people, most people would deduce from the fact that this damn priest is giving the requiem mass that the family considers Yuca guilty of ordering Olga María's murder. There's something very fishy going on, I can tell you that, and I'm going to find out what it is, my dear. This can't just end here; this is one more piece of the whole big plot against Yuca. Maybe Doña Olga is taking part in it without realizing it, innocently, she's so naive and in so much pain, the poor thing. Look at that priest: can't you just see him lowering his eyes and speaking to God, the pig? It makes me want to switch religions. But Papa says they're all the same. He calls himself an agnostic. I've never really understood what that means: something about believing in a God up there, but not in the priests or the religions down here. Papa says he doesn't need the priests' God: he's happy hanging out on his finca most of the time or going a few times a year to the racetrack in Mexico City and to the casinos in Reno; that's what he loves to do. You should see how he makes fun of Mama. He says that all her religious fervour, her devotion to the priests, it all started when she was already old – she never even went to church before; even my first communion was just a formality. He's right: when I was little Mama wasn't at all interested in priests or services, she was on a different wavelength altogether. Fear of death, my dear. According to Papa, the war turned my mother into a zealot, as if God would save her from the massacres, when it was the priests themselves who'd stirred up the masses. That's what Papa says. He makes fun of her, because as far as he's concerned, now that the war is over Mama should give up all her piousness. But she's too old to change now. I understand her. But when you come across disgusting priests like this one here, you can't help having terrible thoughts. I want to see what he pulls out of his hat for the homily. Let's kneel, my dear. This *prie-dieu* is filthy, it's going to ruin my stockings. Did I tell you I had dinner with Marito? Night before last. At his house, so we could be with the girls and dear Julita. He told me a bunch of things, and he questioned me pretty aggressively. Not during dinner, because the girls were there, the poor things, my darlings; no, after they went to bed. Marito's business isn't doing so well: he's lost some clients. He says he's invoicing about sixty per cent of what he invoiced last year. Apparently advertising feels the economic crunch first because it's the first item on the budget that gets cut. That's what Marito explained to me. This crisis is awful, it's affecting everybody, it's all the fault of that fat idiot we put in there as president. Interest rates have even dropped. Luckily the price of coffee has remained stable, if not, Papa would be furious. Let's sit, my dear. What Marito told me is that Olga María didn't leave a will – how could she have imagined she would die so young!? That's why at the beginning of last week I went to a lawyer to write mine, my dear – I hope it doesn't bring bad luck. God forbid. Knock on wood. But there's no problem because the girls inherit everything. Her only partner in the boutique was Doña Olga. They kept things in the family. But Marito isn't sure it's worth keeping the boutique: if you add to the economic crisis the scandal of Olga María's murder, it probably isn't. I asked him what he was planning to do about Cheli and Conchita, the two employees, because I'm sure they're the ones who blabbed to the police. Doña Olga wants to keep them on and Marito couldn't care less. Imagine that. I told him he'd better get rid of that pair of harpies as soon as possible or he'd soon regret it. OK, my dear, I'll keep my voice down, the last thing I want is for that damned priest to tell me off. It's just that when I talk about those you-know-whats, I flip out. The same thing happened when I was with Marito. Luckily dear Julita had already put the girls to bed. They're so lovely, so obedient, such good students. That's what bothers me about going to mass: you have to constantly be standing up, kneeling down, standing up, and my clothes end up getting all messed up and looking frightful. It was because I got so excited when I was talking about Cheli and Conchita that Marito asked me what I have against them; he said they're good employees, Olga María trusted them completely. I'm such an idiot, I went and told him what I suspected: that the two of them had filled the policemen's heads with all sorts of groundless rumours, especially that Deputy Chief Handal. Then I realized I'd stuck my foot in my mouth, but it was too late to turn back. Marito just stared at me with a very serious expression on his face. We were still in the dining room drinking coffee. What rumours? he asked me, in a not very friendly voice. I didn't know what to do, my dear. I probably stared back at him like an idiot, because he asked me again: What rumours? I felt trapped, like he was reading my mind. But finally I managed to wriggle my way out of it: I told him how it could appear suspicious that he bought a life-insurance policy for Olga María a few weeks before the murder. Everybody, of course, thinks it's ridiculous, but those two put it into the policeman's head, and this Deputy Chief Handal questioned me about it. That's how I explained it to Marito. He told me it wasn't a hypothesis, it was pure nonsense, not even the police were taking it seriously. Then, out of the blue, he asked me about the relationship between Olga María and Yuca. I was shocked. I didn't expect that. I was afraid Marito would find out about the photograph José Carlos had taken of Olga María, the one Handal showed me; that's what I was most afraid of. But Marito going straight to the business about Yuca, I never expected that. It's not like him: he's not one for confrontations. That's why he got along so well with Olga María: they were both calm, gentle, reserved. You can't imagine the predicament I was in, my dear. Just look at him there, praying, as gentle as a lamb, but that Marito, he's a sly one, throwing me a curve ball like that. At first I had no idea what to say. All I could do was play the fool, ask him what he was talking about, what was he insinuating. And maybe because it was the second time I'd had to play the fool, I got angry. My head felt like it was about to explode: I told him he couldn't possibly believe all that nonsense those mean-spirited people were gossiping about, Olga María and Yuca had never been anything more than friends, great friends since the American School, I knew that for a fact, Olga María confided in me things she never confided in anybody, and as far as I'm concerned it's utter nonsense for him to entertain any suspicions at all about his wife, about someone who'd always been faithful to him. I almost called him an idiot. I was getting quite worked up, I was shouting, because I wasn't going to let that good-for-nothing doubt her and join the conspiracy against Yuca. I ripped into him: I said those little bitches, Cheli and Conchita, they must have had a hand in telling Deputy Chief Handal the rumours that he's made it his business to spread around. All because Olga María had been receiving phone calls from Yuca the last few weeks of her life. Those hussies think that if somebody gets a phone call from a friend she must be sleeping with him. Just because that's what they're like, them and their sluttish mentality. I'll bet one of them is going out with one of the detectives who works under Deputy Chief Handal and that's where all the rumours are coming from. But I made it very clear to Marito that if recently Yuca had been communicating with Olga María, it was because he was having personal problems and he was reaching out to old friends, lifelong friends, that's why he'd called me, too. I wasn't about to go telling him all of Yuca's problems, those things are private, the poor man has enough problems with all the dirty politics he's messed up in. Marito asked me to calm down, the girls weren't asleep yet and they might be listening. But I was already in a rage – he'd provoked me. I told him I thought it was shameful for him to start questioning his wife's honesty, there wasn't a bit of difference between his insinuations and what other evil tongues were saying about him hiring somebody to kill her. Until I said that, I couldn't calm down! Yes, my dear, I just realized it – I'll lower my voice. Let's kneel again. Did you see that look my mother just shot me when she turned around? I'll pretend I didn't notice. Look at those saints. Perfectly awful. Whose idea was it to dress them up like that? Such poor taste. Not at all like those sculptures you see in the churches in Europe – look at the face on that one. Poor thing. Who knows who he's supposed to be. I've never learnt anything about the saints. Papa says most of them are phoneys or criminals. Mama's hair stands on end when Papa starts ranting and raving against the Pope and the Vatican. All that's for the lower classes, for people who are either stupid or ignorant, Papa says. Speaking of which: neither Cheli nor Conchita came to church. They've already forgotten about Olga María. What I said earlier is true: Cheli is going out with one of Handal's detectives. I know it first-hand, my dear. The one with the square jaw, like a filing cabinet, Villalta I think his name is, he's really got the mug of a criminal, he's the one who came to interrogate the girls right after Olga María was killed. You know which one Cheli is? She's the chubby one with big cheeks, kind of red in the face, very vivacious. It's not her fault she's stupid, but it is her fault people are saying bad things about Olga María. I'll bet you anything she gives Villalta all his leads. I saw them together, that's what I'm telling you, I didn't hear it from anyone. It was pure coincidence. I was walking down Paseo Escalón, about two blocks below Villas Españolas, right near her boutique, when what do you know? I see that disgusting Cheli walking with that detective. I didn't want to tell Marito about it; they'd just say I was gossiping and the woman has a right to have a boyfriend. But can you believe the prize she's found for herself. I told Doña Olga, of course. Just so she'd know. The night before last, with Marito, after he was rude to me and I had to put him in his place, I told him about Cheli and the detective. But we weren't at his house any more. Marito was very upset when I told him that some people were saying that he might have arranged Olga María's murder. I swear he went totally blank for about five seconds; not because he hadn't thought of it or because nobody had mentioned it to him, but because I threw it in his face right when he started making those filthy insinuations about her. All he managed to say was that we shouldn't talk about it, the girls or dear Julita might show up any moment, we should change the subject. Then I suggested we go out, because I had several related issues I wanted to discuss with him, and it didn't seem right to do it in the house. We went to the bar at the

Hotel Fiesta, it's the closest one. We each took our own car, obviously. The last thing I need is for people to start gossiping about how I'm going out with Marito now that Olga María is dead. All I wanted was to speak frankly, and to hear from him who he suspects or blames for her death. You might not believe this, but it's been a month since her murder, and we still hadn't had a heart-to-heart. For a thousand and one reasons. Or maybe we were afraid. Sometimes you just don't want to know, with so much garbage swirling around. But what made me fighting mad was hearing Marito repeat the same lies against Yuca. Well, he didn't come right out and say it, but just the fact that he insinuated it was enough. He's the husband, my dear – anything he says or even hints at becomes the truth. That's why I wanted to keep talking to him, try to clear things up. The bar was empty; nobody ever stays at the hotel itself, at least not during the week. I don't like that hotel. There's a lien on it, because of the owner's debts. But it's the nearest bar. That's why I suggested it to Marito. He probably goes there often, because the staff seemed to know him, especially one waitress, quite attractive, good body, but dark-skinned, ordinary-looking – not ugly, even kind of cute. So, this is what we've come to, I said to Marito, because it was obvious he liked that waitress, maybe he's even gone out with her, otherwise she wouldn't be so friendly. That's what I told him. But he pretended not to understand. Men have no staying power, my dear. His wife just died and here he is running after a waitress. Marito ordered his usual: vodka with lemonade. I didn't feel like deciding, so I ordered the same. Stand up, my dear. Sometimes I feel like an idiot repeating all this drivel. Finally, we can sit down. Let's see what this despicable priest comes up with next; not that I'm even listening to him. Right from the start, I got straight to the point with Marito: I asked him what he knew about the murder investigation, I told him not to beat around the bush, to tell me once and for all what had happened. He looked so sad, it was actually touching: I realized he didn't know anything either, he just has hypotheses like we do, the whole month he'd been flailing around, at the mercy of everyone's wagging tongues, without anything solid to hold on to. Poor thing. Maybe that's why he's clutching at the possibility that Yuca had something to do with the murder. I told him that later. What he told me is that nothing's been proven: the murderer, that Robocop guy, hasn't confessed to anything, he's held his tongue, he doesn't even admit he was the one who pulled the trigger, even though the girls have positively identified him. Times are different now, you can't apply the kind of pressure you could before, because those human-rights communists will jump down your throat. Marito says that this Deputy Chief Handal is pursuing a very discreet line of investigation. Seems Robocop belongs to a well-organized gang of criminals for hire. Marito thinks that if Robocop was a soldier and belongs to a gang there must be at least one high-ranking military officer behind him. I don't understand why a high-ranking military officer would have wanted Olga

María murdered; I don't see the point, unless he wants to become a politico at Yuca's expense. But Marito doesn't have many expectations: he says that if Robocop doesn't spill the beans, which will most likely be the case, we'll never know who hired him. He also doesn't think Deputy Chief Handal is digging deep enough; there are so many murders and most of them remain unsolved. Marito says that the police are satisfied that they've arrested the perpetrator, that in itself is a huge success, that's why they made such a big to-do about it in the media, but he says they don't care about finding the mastermind. I don't doubt it. This is the only prayer I know in full: Our Father. The rest, I just know parts of them. You, too, right, my dear? Well, you studied with nuns, you learnt them when you were little, I didn't learn any of it. What? Am I going to take communion? Are you kidding? If that priest gives it to me, I won't be able to resist the urge to spit it back in his face. Damn him! We have to kneel again; what's going to happen to my stockings? As I was saying, I couldn't get much out of Marito: he doesn't know anything we don't already know. Unless he's a really good liar and he was pulling the wool over my eyes the whole time. You never know with men. You should have seen him flirting with that waitress, like I wasn't even there. He thinks he's God's gift to women, the poor thing. I don't know how Olga María could have married him. That woman's got guts, you know, because Marito might be a really nice guy, but to have to put up with him every day, God help me. It's not that he's ugly, I just don't see anything attractive about him: he's your ordinary dark man. His personality is the only thing worthwhile: he's calm, kind, generous. That's why Olga María agreed to marry him – they were meant for each other. I can't imagine them screaming at each other, much less fighting. But as much of a goodie-two-shoes as Marito is, he kept on flirting with that waitress until I told him to get a grip, he was going way overboard, showing me no respect, like I was a rag doll or something. So he cooled down. That's when I insisted he tell me everything he knows, not to keep any secrets, I was Olga María's best friend, and he had no reason to hide anything from me. I stared right at him and looked very serious, just so he'd understand that I wasn't joking, the best thing would be to stop keeping secrets from me. He told me that Diana, her younger sister, had hired a private detective, while she was still in Miami, someone named Pepe Pindonga, just like it sounds even though it sounds like a joke, his name is Pepe Pindonga, some kind of weirdo who's already questioned Marito and already started snooping around. Diana's the only one who would have thought of doing such a thing: hiring a private detective, like this is the States or something. She's nuts. Can you imagine, my dear? A private detective in San Salvador? All he'll do is take her money and run. But, anyway, that's her business not mine. Marito warned me not to be surprised if this Pepe Pindonga tries to get in touch with me. It seems he's an ordinary-looking guy, a bit vulgar, who asks questions with no consideration, like he belongs to the same social class or something. I don't want to have anything to do with him. I told Marito that's all I need: some charlatan who calls himself a private detective coming and treating me without respect, as if I haven't already had enough with that Deputy Chief Handal and his gang. I told him I wasn't willing to be questioned by a private detective, I have absolutely no interest in talking to somebody who will probably use whatever information we give him to blackmail us, only someone as demented as Diana could think there's such a thing as a private detective in this city. Marito says the guy is intelligent, clever, but he agrees that Diana is throwing her money away, because if we're dealing with an organized gang of former military officers, this detective will resign from the case in a second. Which doesn't mean he won't charge Diana, even if he hasn't accomplished anything. That's what I think, anyway. We drank three vodkas each. Marito wanted to keep drinking, but I told him it was late, I felt pretty sloshed, and the truth is, I wasn't enjoying myself, and least of all when I had to constantly remind Marito not to flirt with that waitress. Look at that, Señor Saint up here is going to sweeten our ears with his homily, he's going to offer us his spiritual and moral teachings. What a swine. I refuse to listen to him. Hypocrite. After what he's done to Yuca, he has the nerve to stand behind the pulpit and speak in the name of God. Have you ever seen such barefaced hypocrisy? Anyway, the thing is, my dear, the only thing I got clear is that Marito's as confused as we are. Maybe the only ones who know anything are the police, but if some ex-officer is involved we'll never find out anything. Oh, and I forgot: there's some journalist who's also investigating the Olga María case, a reporter from that newspaper, *Ocho Columnas*. Can you believe it? That rag that only reports scandals – the very same newspaper that's been waging its campaign against Yuca, that's been harassing him for weeks. And you know who the famous reporter is? That pathetic creature named Rita Mena, the same one who accused Yuca of assaulting her, as if she wasn't asking for it with her stupid questions. Haven't you read the newspapers, about the journalist union's accusations against Yuca? They say that Yuca and his bodyguards intimidated the reporter, assaulted her – she claimed they grabbed her camera away so they could destroy the roll of film with the pictures she'd taken of Yuca. That's the same reporter who's investigating the murder. It infuriates me. I suspect it's precisely Yuca's enemies who are behind that newspaper, the same ones who launched that press campaign to oust him from the party leadership, the same ones who made that huge fuss about the stolen car this shameless priest sold him, the ones who sent that reporter to Yuca just to provoke him. I don't even want to think about what she'll write about Olga María's death. I can already imagine it. Yuca's enemies want that stupid woman to implicate him in the murder. I'm sure of it. Marito was the one who told me that reporter has been harassing him for the last few days. I don't know how she found out about my existence, because she told Marito she wants to interview me. I'm just waiting for her to call me, my dear, so I can tell her to go straight to hell. She'll get what's coming to her, for snooping around, for being stupid. Did that priest finally finish with his bullshit? I don't believe you're going to take communion. Me? Are you kidding?

6. The Terrace

Luckily I found you, my dear. I made up my mind to stop by your house once and for all to tell you all about it. Nobody else is home, right? Thank goodness. Bring me a glass of water, I'm very agitated. You wouldn't believe what happened to me, what I've found out. Such a scoop. Let's go out on the terrace: there's a nice breeze. Yes, I'm in shock. It's something you wouldn't believe. Try to guess. It's got to do with Olga María. You can't guess, can you? Are you ready, my dear: apparently Olga María and Alberto had an *affaire*. Yes, my ex-husband, if you can believe it. I'm going to tell you everything, blow by blow. Settle in, because it's a long story. I love how you can see the city from up here, especially at this time of day, when the sun has already set. The chaise longue turned out so pretty with that printed fabric. Well, the thing is, this morning I went to Mercedes's beauty salon to get my hair done. Do you like how it turned out? I told her to straighten the ends, like Turlington wears it, that model from the States – though they say her mother is Salvadorean, but who knows what kind of family it is. Anyway, I was at the beauty salon for about an hour, chatting with Mercedes – she's really nice. At some point, I don't know when, we started talking about Olga María. Mercedes loved her a lot. She's been doing our hair for ten years. I don't understand why you've never wanted to give her a try.

Anyway, the thing is that, while we were talking about Olga María, I sensed a change in Mercedes's voice, a different tone, like there was something she didn't want to talk about, or like she had something to hide. I was flipping through a magazine. But then I looked up and saw Mercedes in the mirror, and something had changed, she had a completely different expression on her face. She realized that I'd realized. You know what I mean? Something weird was going on. Since I don't know how to keep things to myself, I asked her what was wrong. She turned her back to me and asked me why I was asking, she said nothing was wrong, other than that she got really sad whenever she thought of Olga María. But sadness isn't what I'd seen in her face: she knew something she didn't want to tell me – that's my intuition, my dear. You know I'm not paranoid. Maybe it made such a strong impression on me because I'd never thought that Mercedes might know something about Olga María's death: she was only her hairdresser, like she's mine. The point is, she was anxious to change the subject, and I couldn't keep insisting, mainly because she had other clients waiting, and one of them was Inés Murillo, who is such a busybody – I don't like her at all. The whole thing left me with a bad feeling. This terrace is so refreshing. No, my dear, no, thank you, I've already had enough coffee. But that's only the very beginning; the best part happened afterwards, when I'd left the beauty salon and was about to get into my car. Can you guess? I had a flat tyre. I was mad as hell. Those things always happen to me at the worst possible moments.

I was about to go back to Mercedes and call the Automobile Club when this person suddenly appeared: he
came right up to me and told me not to worry, he'd change
my tyre. I was suspicious. I said, thank you very much, but
I don't want to bother you, I'll call the Automobile Club,
and they'll send somebody out. The guy was adamant: he
told me I would waste more than an hour waiting for the
Automobile Club truck to come, he was a member, too,
and he'd had a similar experience a few weeks ago. I
checked the man out more carefully: he didn't look like a
hooligan, though these days one can never be sure, but
also there was a guard with a huge machine gun right
across the street at the mall. That's why I figured I wasn't
risking anything, and there was no question he'd change
the tyre long before anybody from the Automobile Club
showed up. When he saw me hesitating, he took off his
blue linen jacket and walked around to the back of the
car, then he motioned to me to open the trunk so he could
get out the tools and the spare tyre. He's dark, short, he's
got an ordinary-enough-looking face, and he was wearing
khakis and a white polo shirt and those Bostonian shoes
everybody and his brother wears. I told myself he'd just
happened to be walking by and he wanted to be chivalrous
and maybe ask me out for a date afterwards. You know
how men are, my dear. We don't expect them to do
something like that for nothing. And I was right. He
hadn't even finished changing the tyre when he started
staring at me: he had this look of surprise on his face, as
if he knew me from somewhere and had just then

recognized me. I expected him to come out with something stupid, like those idiots who say, "Haven't we met somewhere before?" but then he asked me if I was Laura Rivera. I stood there staring at him, very serious and not very friendly, I felt like asking him what it was to him who I was, don't be so nosy, just change the tyre, which anyway I'd never even asked him to do, he's the one who insisted on helping me with who knows what ulterior motives; I even had the urge to tell him to get away from my car immediately, don't touch it again, or my tyres, or my tools, go, get lost now, I'll call the Automobile Club like I should have from the get-go. I was about to walk over to the security guard and ask him to watch my car very carefully and make sure that man leaves it exactly as it is while I go to Mercedes's salon to use the phone, I was on the verge of blowing up over the nerve of that dark, fat-lipped dwarf, when he mentioned Olga María. This is what he said: that I was best friends with Doña Olga María de Trabanino, he recognized me from several photos he'd seen at her house, photos Don Mario – that's what he called him – had been kind enough to show him. The man spoke quickly: he didn't give me a chance to get a word in edgeways, and I could tell he was trying to make a good impression. It made me furious to think that Marito's the only person I know who'd even think of going around showing pictures to the first person who asked to see them. Then the man said what a coincidence it was: he was on his way to the beauty salon to interview Mercedes, and here he'd run into me, how fortunate, fate was clearly on his side. That was when I realized who I was dealing with: he had to be that detective Diana hired and Marito told me about. On top of it, his nose looked like a fried egg. I was incensed, it was obvious this guy had been looking for a chance to meet me; I got the feeling there was much more than met the eye behind this supposedly chance encounter. But just then he held out his hand and told me his name was Pepe Pindonga, it was an honour to have this opportunity to meet me, several people had spoken very highly of me. I was about to tell him to get lost, make yourself scarce, but my curiosity got the better of me, my desire to find out why this detective had decided to question Mercedes, so I didn't send him on his way right then and there. I like this terrace, and if you had a drop of something to drink, now that things have cooled off, it would be fantastic; yes, I'd love a shot of Kahlúa. While he was putting the tools away in the trunk and sweating like crazy, I asked him, pretending I was just curious. He told me that one of his hypotheses in the case – that's what he said, "hypotheses", as if he were Deputy Chief Handal himself – had led him right to this beauty salon I had just left. I wanted to tell him that it seemed like a dirty trick for a phoney like him, a charlatan who passes himself off as a private detective, to try to implicate a working woman like Mercedes in Olga María's murder. But this Pepe Pindonga didn't let me talk, he was irrepressible, vehement, gesturing wildly, it was like the world was about to come to an end and he had to utter the most number of words in the least amount of time possible. He told me it wouldn't be appropriate for us to discuss such a delicate subject there in the parking lot, he would very much like to talk to me in private, try to corroborate some information he had, and he'd be delighted to tell me all about his hypothesis about the beauty salon if I'd accept his invitation to go with him to have a cup of coffee. This Pepe Pindonga doesn't beat around the bush, my dear; he's dangerous, he swallows you up, as if he were a hypnotist or a magician. At some point, I don't know when, he'd got into my car and sat down next to me, then he asked me to put the air conditioning on full blast otherwise he'd never stop sweating. The guy is like a machine gun, he doesn't stop talking, and about any subject whatsoever: he said he loves BMWs, he's a great admirer of these cars, even though he's never had one, but at one point in his career as a journalist he worked for a magazine about automobiles, that's why he knows so much about them and nobody can get anything past him. I had to force him to be quiet so I could ask him where we were going. Mercedes's beauty salon is in the Balam Quitzé mall, as you know, that's why he suggested we go to the Hotel El Salvador; that was the nearest place. I wasn't so sure about it: I didn't relish the prospect of walking with that guy into a place where I'd probably run into more than one person I knew, but I couldn't think of any place else to go, and I wanted to hear all about the Mercedes connection. This Pepe Pindonga should be a radio announcer instead of a private detective: in that short ride to the hotel he managed to tell me a huge chunk of his life story. During the war he lived in Mexico, where he worked as a reporter for one of the major newspapers there. He told me how one time he came to San Salvador to do a report on the bizarre suicide of a captain in the armed forces, a squalid story that implicated several other officers and resulted in Pepe Pindonga having to make a quick getaway to avoid being killed. That was during the war, according to him. He was telling me all this on our way to the hotel, and I wasn't paying much attention because all I wanted to know was about Olga María's case and his hypothesis about Mercedes. But I couldn't figure out how to make him shut up. He told me he came back to live here a few months after the war ended, when Cristiani had already surrendered to the terrorists, as Papa says. He worked for a while at *Ocho Columnas*. Can you believe it? Yes, indeed, my dear, the very same newspaper that waged the campaign against Yuca. I was in shock when he said that. The first thought that came to me was that this big-mouthed phoney was part of the conspiracy against Yuca. I was about to put him in his place, demand that he get out of my car immediately, when he asked me if I knew Rita Mena, the reporter from the same newspaper who was in charge of investigating Olga María's murder. That was the last straw. I told him I didn't, I told him I had absolutely no interest in meeting that kind of trash, I consider journalists to be a filthy race, buzzards, vultures after carrion, flies hovering over shit – and that stupid reporter from *Ocho Columnas* more than any of them, I consider her an accomplice in the plot against Yuca, and it's only because I've got good manners that I'd give him a ride back to the mall because I had nothing more to say to him. He told me to take it easy, not to get the wrong idea: he hated *Ocho Columnas*, too, everybody who works there, and especially Rita Mena; it was her fault he'd had to leave that paper, he could deliver truckloads of dirt on that sleazebag. He convinced me to keep driving to the hotel when he told me he was certain that Rita Mena and the newspaper had been involved in a bigger conspiracy aimed at removing Yuca from the political arena. The way he said it, it sounded like he was repeating my very own words. He has absolutely no doubt that Olga María's murder is being used to finish Yuca off. His words. If the case is rigorously investigated the clues will lead to those who have been the main beneficiaries of Yuca's political demise. I was stunned, my dear, that was precisely what I was thinking but I hadn't been able to put into so many words, plus I realized that this detective knew a lot. You know what else he said? That only an idiot or someone with ulterior motives would think that Yuca or another one of her lovers would've had Olga María murdered; we're dealing here with a crime committed for perfectly calculated political motives, not a crime of passion, like that Deputy Chief Handal is trying to make us believe. Precisely what I think. I managed to ask him if he'd spoken about all this and in such clear terms to Marito. He told me they were paying him to investigate the murder, not sink a recently widowed man into a deep depression; if he was telling me this, it was because he was sure I already knew about Olga María's escapades. "Escapades", the moron said, like she was some kind of floozy. Luckily, when I got to the hotel I didn't see anybody I knew, and in the café I chose a corner table and sat with my back to the entrance. I love how they remodelled that hotel; it looks so modern, so spacious, everything's in such good taste. I like the architecture of the boutiques the best. Did you know that when they first started the remodel they asked Olga María if she wanted to open up a branch of her boutique there? But she thought it was too risky. The thing is, once we were sitting in the café, I asked him how he'd found out about Yuca and Olga María's relationship. He told me that when they threw him out of *Ocho Columnas*, he went to work as the head of PR for the police academy. Can you imagine the contacts he established there? He's made a lot of progress in the investigation. He told me a ton of things. Supposedly, we were just going for a cup of coffee, but we talked for about four hours; first in the café, then we went to the bar, and then we ate at the restaurant next to the pool. He doesn't drink coffee or alcohol or smoke; the exact opposite of the private detectives in the movies. He says he's already used up his quota of drinking and smoking, he's already ingested enough toxins for a lifetime. He doesn't look that old to me at all, but who knows what kind of life he's led. He ordered a camomile tea and I had a Coca-Cola. Then he told me that Diana had hired him totally out of the blue, he's never met her, all he's seen is a photo Marito showed him; they've spoken on the telephone, it would be ridiculous if they hadn't at least done that. He says about fifteen days ago he received a fax in his office, near Bloom Hospital, next to the university, in that area, I'm not sure exactly where, I get lost in that neighbourhood. The fax was from Diana in Miami, requesting his services to investigate the murder of Olga María. Diana doesn't trust the police. He claims he doesn't know how Diana heard about him and decided to hire him. But he immediately plunged into the case. He's had access to the police reports, he says, and I believe him, my dear, because he knows more than we do: he mentioned Olga María's relationship with Julio Iglesias, with José Carlos, with Yuca. Then I went totally numb when he asked me if I knew that my ex-husband had had an *affaire* with her. It took me so much by surprise that I didn't know what to say. I still haven't digested it fully. Can you imagine Olga María finding Alberto attractive? I simply can't make head nor tail of it. That's what I told the detective when I came out of my state of shock: I told him he'd have to show me some proof if he wanted me to believe him, it was some kind of misunderstanding, malicious gossip cooked up by the police. And I couldn't even manage to get angry because suddenly I was putting two and two together. Pepe Pindonga was categorical – the man is heartless: he told me that Olga María and Alberto had met at least a couple of times before we got divorced. Imagine that! What a fool I was not to have realized it. He went on to explain that the first time was at Olga María's, the morning after a party, when you-know-who returned to the house with the excuse that he'd left

124

his sweater there, and they took advantage of nobody being home; the other time Alberto picked her up at the beauty salon. That's why Mercedes got so nervous when I started talking about Olga María, because the detective had just been there questioning her and got that information out of her. Then, while my brain was working a million miles a minute, I began to catch a glimpse of what the beauty-salon "hypothesis" consisted of. I was determined to have the answers. He said, yes, Alberto's name appeared in a report about the investigation into her lovers, especially because he's been managing Olga María's and her family's finances. By this time, my dear, we were in the bar, so I ordered a double whiskey. He said he'd talked enough, he'd told me everything he knew, now it was my turn, I needed to help him, tell him everything I knew so we could work together and that way he could move his investigation forwards. He mainly asked me about what you already know, but in much greater detail than the police. The horrible part is that the more I talked the more I realized that this man was only looking to confirm what he already knew; I wasn't, in fact, telling him anything new, just corroborating the information in the police reports he'd read and the inquiries he'd carried out on his own. The truth is, I was feeling pretty distressed, choked up and all, because of the Alberto thing, and I wanted to get back to that, hear more about the relationship between my ex-husband and Olga María. Weird, because I didn't feel angry, none of that rage that blinds you when you feel like you've been betrayed, but instead there was this sadness, anxiety, as if suddenly nothing made any sense. That's why I wasn't responding with much enthusiasm and Pepe Pindonga had to pry everything out of me. There was a moment, around when I ordered a second drink, that I felt like crying, I swear, that's how I felt, because I'd always been so loyal to Olga María, and now it turns out she didn't show me any consideration at all. Pepe noticed my state of mind – he's very sensitive – and he said maybe it'd be better to change the subject; he saw me so sad, he hadn't wanted to hurt me, but it was better for me to know so I wouldn't hear about it later and be even more shocked. He tried to comfort me: Olga María didn't want to hurt me by getting involved with Alberto, she probably didn't have any control over those unconscious urges that made her have sex with men, I knew her better than anybody else did and should forgive her. Pepe Pindonga said all that. I couldn't control myself any longer and I shed a tear, then another, and another; it all happened in silence, with no big fuss, a mournful cry, melancholic, like I was remembering somebody I'd lost a long time ago. Luckily, it's pretty dark in the hotel bar and the TV's always on, so nobody knew what was happening to me, only Pepe: he took my hand and squeezed it. It's pretty awful, my dear, to find out about something like that. With my last glimmer of hope I asked him about his sources, how he'd got his information. But Pepe had already warned me that he wasn't going to reveal any names. All I can guess is, other than Mercedes, maybe Julita, Olga María's housekeeper, maybe she

126

confided in her, or those blabbermouths Cheli and Conchita, who work at the boutique. Who knows? It's unbelievable how you can live, being deceived by your best friend and your husband. Though I couldn't care less about Alberto; on the contrary, he must have something going for him besides his money-making ability, otherwise our friend wouldn't have got involved with him. Bring me some more water, my dear, my mouth is dry from talking so much. I don't want to get sad again, especially on this overcast afternoon. But I'm telling you, I'm going to call Alberto later tonight when he gets home from the office, I don't want him to think I'm a total imbecile, to think they can cheat on me like that and me not have a clue. Pepe Pindonga advised me not to: why dig up dirt from such a long time ago? But I'm not going to repress myself. That's what I told him when we'd already gone to eat at the restaurant by the pool; Alberto's going to pay for this. You'd keep your mouth shut, wouldn't you? So what if we got divorced a long time ago. Pepe says maybe Olga María seduced him – but no man goes to bed with a woman by force. He's a wolf in sheep's clothing, and the same goes for Olga María. Pepe told me he's trying to create a psychological profile of her – it would help his investigation – because even though he's almost a hundred per cent sure that the murder was planned to hurt Yuca, one should never completely neglect other lines of investigation. He told me that my name appears in the police reports as a possible suspect, because of the *affaire* between Alberto and Olga María and my connections with Yuca. Can you believe it? I got indignant, my dear. Not only do I have to swallow the fact that my best friend slept with my ex-husband but also that they suspect me of having her killed. It's unbelievable. I was so angry I lost my appetite. I had the urge to immediately call that Deputy Chief Handal and read him the riot act. But Pepe tried to calm me down: I wasn't a suspect in the strict sense of the word, it's just that I'm considered part of secondary investigations, offshoots, ones that feed into and support the central inquiry. No matter what, it's outrageous. Now, after thinking about it a lot, I disagree with Pepe Pindonga: I believe Olga María went to bed with Alberto fully conscious of what she was doing. She was perverse, my dear, it all started when I told her that my relationship with Alberto was on the rocks, he was useless in bed, life with him was the most boring thing that could ever happen to me; that's all she needed to hear to decide she wanted to give him a whirl. That's what I think. She wanted to try him out to see if what I told her was true or not. Simply perverse. Most likely she found out I wasn't lying, because Pepe Pindonga assures me that he has dependable information about only a couple of encounters. My head hasn't stopped racing all afternoon, my dear. Horrible: I've had the most awful thoughts. I haven't had a moment of peace. Now I feel a little calmer. Your house really is in the best part of the city: you have a gorgeous view, it's super-cool here, and it's not that far away from shopping and everything else you need. You know what I've even started thinking? That Alberto hurried the divorce through

– even though I was the one who first suggested it – because he had hopes of starting up something with Olga María. It's not paranoia, my dear. All of them were ready to separate from their wives in order to be with her. Why would Alberto, who was sort of dense about things like that, be the exception? I might be exaggerating, you might be right, but by now anything seems possible. It's as if I just got rudely awoken with a slap across the face. What a nightmare. The worst part is that there I was, accomplice and confidante in all her romances: I feel cheated, and idiotic. I'm going to get even with that piece of shit Alberto, and I'm going to force him to confess everything, absolutely everything, the whole nine yards. Who does that idiot think he is? The good part is that this Pepe Pindonga is a great conversationalist, he knows an infinite number of stories, and when he saw how distraught I was, he changed the subject to get me to calm down. He started telling me about something super-interesting: his experiences at some kind of school of the esoteric. He said he was in some kind of monastery, in the mountains in central Mexico, where the masters are old indigenous people who've experimented with hallucinogenic mushrooms. He asked me if I'd been in Mexico. I told him only briefly: Papa hates that country, he says Mexicans are thieves and bums, and the Aztecs were barbarians. That's why I've never been very interested; I prefer to go to Miami or New York. Don't you feel the same way? The thing is that there we were, the detective and I chatting away, right next to the pool, hanging around after dinner, about to have coffee or tea. I don't know how we got back to the subject of Rita Mena, the reporter. He told me that she'd accused him of sexual harassment and that's why his situation at the newspaper deteriorated to the point where he had to resign. Seems like that girl blows everything out of proportion, she's a compulsive liar, ever since she covered that story about the snakes; do you remember that huge scandal, about that maniac in a yellow Chevrolet full of snakes who went around terrorizing the population a few years ago? She thinks she's the cat's miaow, but she's just a nobody, that's why anybody can easily manipulate her, like they did to wage their campaign against Yuca. Now she's trying to get in to interview that Robocop criminal so she can write an article that will earn her one of those journalism prizes the priests hand out. That's what Pepe Pindonga told me. But it seems Robocop plays his cards very close; that man's kept his lips zipped, that's why they hired him. Oh, dear, it's getting late. It's so pleasant here on the terrace, but I can't stand it any longer, I have to call Alberto. He's going to be so surprised, this Olga María case is getting uglier all the time. I get the impression nobody has found the unifying thread. You can tell that Pepe Pindonga is no simpleton, but even he admitted there comes a point where all the trails go cold. By the way, he asked me about you. Yes, Pepe did, about if you had been a good friend of Olga María's, where you work, how much I trust you; the man is nosy, I'm warning you. I told him I was sick of being interrogated, you are one of my best friends, and you weren't about to go gossiping about me. But he wouldn't take no for an answer. I wouldn't be surprised if he decided to interview you. He's nice enough. We left it that we'd meet again in a few days. He said he'd get in touch with me, even though he also left me his card. Here it is in case you're interested. I bet you'll run into him when you least expect to, like I did, but once he gets hold of you he doesn't let go. You know I even got to thinking that the sly fox probably let the air out of my tyre. Too much of a coincidence, my dear. I can't trust anybody any more.

7. The Crash

I couldn't wait to call you, my dear, things are heating up so fast. I talked to Alberto, about an hour ago, as soon as I got back from your house. I gave him a piece of my mind about the disgusting things he did with Olga María. I had no intention of even letting him defend himself, all I wanted to do was throw in his face everything Pepe Pindonga told me. And that's just what I did: I told him he was a son of a bitch, a real bastard, how dare he betray his friendship with Marito and my trust; how dare he make a mockery of our best friends' marriage. I guaranteed him this was not going to be the end of it, I'd get even with him, he'd better watch his step. I caught him completely off guard, he wasn't expecting anything of the sort, and I didn't let him answer or get a word in edgeways. I didn't hold back: you pig, I said, you slept with my best friend, you betrayed every principle in the book, you took advantage of all of us, we all trusted you. I even told him he was going to die. I threatened him, just so he'd know it wasn't all just hot air: Marito is going to hear about this, and your family, I told him, and my mother and my father, I'm going to tell everybody. The cherry on top was to warn him that the police suspect him, maybe he ordered Olga María's murder so he could cover up the disgusting things he'd done with her and so that neither Marito or I would find out, so he could stay in good with Olga María's family and mine. I don't know why I said that, my dear, but suddenly I realized it actually could be true, come to think of it, one of the many hypotheses could point to Alberto as a suspect. I told him that, and also that I wouldn't be at all surprised to find out that he'd had Olga María murdered, that's when I stopped to take a deep breath. I was exhausted, panting, I expected Alberto to start mumbling some excuses or maybe even denying in a really cynical way that he'd had sexual relations with Olga María. But Alberto didn't react: I didn't hear a peep from the other end of the line, as if he'd put the phone down on the table and left the room. Then I shouted at him not to be such a coward, to say something, admit he'd been a pig, a hypocrite, and in the end everything had turned out badly for him because he'd pushed through our divorce hoping he could be with Olga María, that's what I shouted at him, now I understood his last-minute rush, what a beast, though mostly just a fool, as if he didn't know Olga María, as if she'd want to separate from Marito so she could be with the most boring man in the world, the worst man on the entire planet Earth to have sex with, an idiot who all he does is go to bed in his undershirt and underwear and wait for someone to climb on top of him, and she'd only do that because she wanted a little relief from the worst case of boredom ever. I ripped into him again, my dear, until I felt I had nothing left in me. Again, I stopped, panting, to catch my breath. That's when I realized he was still on the other end of the line, listening to me. I thought he'd hung up, but no: he barely mumbled something about me being unfair. Can you believe it? Me, unfair, to him? Stupid fool. I was about to take off on another rant, really put him in his place, tell him that fairness is something between human beings, not animals, when all of a sudden he exploded, hysterical – it was incredible, I've never heard such frenzy in his voice – he started shrieking uncontrollably, saying I should quit bothering him with trifles like this gossip about Olga María, it's totally inconsequential compared to the catastrophe that's befallen him, a catastrophe that will land him in jail or murdered. Then he let it all out: Finapro is bankrupt. Imagine that. Dreadful, my dear. The financial company has gone bankrupt. That's what he said. All the money's gone to hell. I still can't believe it. Alberto is the vice president – if he says so, it must be true. He was beside himself. He told me that instead of haranguing him with ridiculous lies about Olga María, I should be helping him, the police were on their way to arrest him. He told me the whole thing was Toñito Rathis's fault. Now that guy, he's insane, my dear, he wants to be president of everything: Finapro, all his family businesses, the government party, the soccer team and, needless to say, the country. That's what Alberto told me, that Toñito made a horrible mess of everything, he used the money from the company to cover losses in other family businesses, to finance the party's election campaign and to pay for his obsession, the soccer team. Imagine that, my dear. Tomorrow the scandal is going to be all over the newspapers. Alberto is dying of fear. They've lost more than a billion colones – incredible – more than a hundred million dollars. Do you realize what that means? This will be the end of everything. Almost everybody I know put their money in Finapro – thousands and millions of colones. Alberto started snivelling on the phone: he said that he'll end up being the fall guy, Toñito Rathis still thinks he's untouchable, after all, he belongs to one of the country's top fourteen families. Poor Alberto, I really felt sorry for him. He told me he can't leave the country, they've already got a policeman on guard in front of his house, he even told me our telephone conversation was probably being taped. Total paranoia, but now for good reason. I asked him what was going to happen to people who had their money invested in Finapro. He said he doesn't know, most likely they'll lose it, the whole thing's gone to hell. Atrocious. Then I thought of Doña Olga: her money's invested in Finapro, and Olga María's too, and probably Marito's. That's when I stopped feeling sorry for him and I asked him, now with anger, what was going to happen to Olga María's family's money, the girls' inheritance, the interest Doña Olga lives on. You know what he told me? It's out of his hands, they are just one of many families affected by the crash, most of his friends have their money in Finapro. He's afraid he'll get killed because several retired military officers, the ones who made millions during the war, also had their money there. He kept ticking off names of people we know who've lost all their savings, all in that same hysterical voice I'd never heard before, like he was about to have a nervous breakdown, but I was already angry as hell, my dear, most of all because I know that Doña Olga invested all the money she got from selling her fincas in Finapro, and I thought about my beautiful little girls, who from one day to the next are going to be left without any inheritance, and then I didn't feel sorry at all for that disgusting Alberto, not only was he a crook but also a fool and a coward – and incompetent. I flew at him in a rage: I shouted at him that he was a fiend, I hope they do kill him for being such a bastard, for thinking he's so high and mighty, the country's leading financier, and look what he's ended up doing with other people's money. Here's what I told him: what good has it done you to get those graduate degrees in the States, you idiot? I warned him that he better recover the money for Olga María's family because if he doesn't, I am personally going to eliminate him. That's when the idiot hung up on me. Which made me even more furious. I dialled him again several times, but it was busy; he must have left the phone off the hook. Then I called his cell. When he heard my voice, he started up again in his fit of hysteria: I should stop bothering him with my nonsense – that's what he said – he was waiting for urgent phone calls and couldn't waste his time on me. He hung up again without giving me a chance to tell him what was on my mind, to say all the horrible things I was thinking about him, because it just can't be that all that money's been lost, money doesn't just disappear from one day to the next, between him and that Toñito Rathis, they must have stolen it, they probably snuck it out of the country and are now acting like they're the victims, pretending the financial company just crashed on its own. Damn thieves. I'm very worried, my dear. So many people are going to lose their money. I immediately called Papa at the finca to tell him. He told me he'd been expecting this, it was impossible for them to be paying twenty-two per cent annually when the banks were paying ten, there had to be something shady going on. That's my father, my dear, sometimes I criticize him for being too conservative, but in the end he always ends up being right. You remember when he warned us against putting our money there when everybody else was going on and on about how Finapro was the very best? I wouldn't have done it anyway, just to avoid having anything to do with Alberto. We did the right thing, my dear. Now I remember that I warned Olga María, told her what Papa told me, but she ignored me, she said it was just my prejudices against Alberto. But here you have the consequences. She was too innocent, she let herself be led down the garden path, she must have totally trusted Alberto, and seeing as how she'd already slept with him, everything seemed under control. What a brilliant way to lose the money they got for the fincas Don Sergio left them. It makes me so mad. I told Papa what I'd talked to Alberto about, the tragedy of Doña Olga and the girls, I asked him if something couldn't be done; it's simply unheard of that suddenly one day Doña Olga will be out on the streets. I wanted to know what Papa thought before I called Doña Olga, because I was certain Alberto hadn't called her, coward that he is. Papa told me that if

Alberto couldn't do anything, nobody else could, either. He repeated that even though he didn't have any evidence, this bankruptcy smelt to him like a gigantic fraud, a tidal wave of shit that was going to bury half the country, and Alberto more than anybody, that's what Papa said. Thank God I separated from that imbecile, and I have absolutely nothing to do with him. Just imagine the mess I'd be in. I don't know why I thought to tell my Papa my suspicions about Alberto and his connection to Olga María's murder. You know how much I trust my father. That's why I told him everything, down to the last detail, just like Pepe Pindonga told me. He was quiet for a while, like he was thinking, then with great concern in his voice he suggested that, because it's such a serious accusation, I should keep it in reserve. But I have this intuition that Alberto's got something to do with our friend's death, and this might just be the connecting thread that will tie up all the loose ends. That's what I thought at that moment, still fuming against Alberto, and here's how I communicated it to Papa: What if Olga María and Alberto were still seeing each other and she found out what was happening with Finapro? Papa just kept repeating that I shouldn't talk about this to anybody else. After I hung up, after all the excitement of having solved the case, I got paralysed. It was like I saw a blinding light. I felt this terrible dread, as if my discovery, that I'd solved the case, could cost me my life. I didn't want to keep thinking. So, instead, I called Doña Olga. Sergio answered. I asked him if he knew about the crisis at Finapro. He told me he did, word had already reached everybody who has their money there, and Doña Olga is falling apart, her blood pressure is shooting sky high, they were waiting for the doctor. I called about half an hour ago. I'm extremely worried, my dear. Can you imagine losing all your money a month and a half after they kill your daughter? Horrible. I'm afraid something serious will happen to Doña Olga, a heart attack or something like that. You know, when things like this happen, people want to die. I asked Sergio if he had his money in that company, too. He said luckily he didn't, but Marito did and a ton of other people did, too. You know who could lose millions, my dear? Yuca. That's what Sergio said: even the archbishop, the Spanish one Papa can't stand, he put the church's money in Finapro. What a disaster Alberto has got himself into. Because he's an imbecile, that's why, a conceited, spoilt brat. Yuca is going to kill him, no doubt about that. Sergio told me people are very upset, they don't know what to do; neither he nor Marito have been able to get hold of Alberto to get some kind of explanation. I told him what he'd said, the situation is now out of his hands, most likely the money can't be recovered. My poor little girls: they've lost their inheritance. I'm telling you, when I hung up, my head was racing a million miles a minute. You know what I mean? That sensation that you're on the verge of discovering something very very important, the pieces are beginning to fall into place. Do you see the threesome? Alberto, Olga María, Yuca. I thought I should call Pepe Pindonga right away. But it was as if that man was reading my mind, because just as I was about to pick up the phone to dial, it rang. Bingo: it was him. I told him about the financial scandal. He told me he already knew, everybody was talking about it, the newspapers were about to print the story, and he'd got all the details from his contacts who'd called him. Then I told him all about my conversation with Alberto, the money Olga María's family had lost, and also the rumours about Yuca having a big portion of his money in that company. He confessed to me that he hadn't known that last bit, and he said that it made the situation much trickier than he'd imagined. I told him straight out my suspicions: that Olga María's murder probably had something to do with Finapro's crash. The more I think about it, the more convinced I get, my dear. You-know-who must have figured out the dirty game Alberto and Toñito Rathis were playing and that's why they decided to get rid of her. Alberto probably opened his big mouth, wanting to impress Olga María – just to show you how stupid he is – and when they realized she was romantically involved with Yuca, they decided to eliminate her. It's the only logical explanation. It scares me, as you can imagine. Of course they're capable of that, and worse: they've stolen billions of colones. Do me a favour! You think they're going to think twice about putting a contract out on someone? That Toñito Rathis is the worst, he's a gangster, my dear, ever since he was at the American School, you could see what a scoundrel he was, even if he was three years ahead of us, he already had quite a reputation. But you know what Pepe Pindonga, the great detective, told me? That my hypothesis sounded very far-fetched to him, there was no evidence to back it up, I must be upset by what's going on, and that's why I keep coming up with these bizarre hypotheses. What an imbecile. I told him I don't have a hypothesis, that hypotheses are for the police or detectives like him, people who aren't interested in finding out the truth because what they really want is to stretch out the investigation for as long as possible so they can keep collecting their wages. He asked me not to get so worked up, it wasn't such a big deal. That made me even more upset: I shouted at him that now that we finally had a solid lead, something that made some sense of Olga María's murder, now that we finally have the chance to solve the case, Mr Smartypants starts putting on airs, doubting what's completely obvious, instead of offering some ideas of his own, instead of taking his own steps to solve it. So I threatened him: he'd better get moving or I'll call Diana in Miami and tell her to fire him for his feeble-minded approach. That's what I told him. I zeroed in on the most important fact that everybody knows: Toñito Rathis wants to take over the party so he can become the candidate for president. My dear, it's the talk of the town, at the Club, everywhere. Papa told me that the one who's benefited most from Yuca's fall from grace is Toñito Rathis; at the next party convention he'll try to become the finance secretary and then the candidate. Do you get it? It's all so clear to me. That idiot Pepe Pindonga, doubting it all. He asked me how it could be possible, if Yuca and Toñito Rathis are enemies, that Yuca

144

invested his money in the other's company. I told him he's a poor slob who doesn't understand anything about business, money is one thing and politics is another, if Finapro was paying out twenty-two per cent annually, anybody would have placed their money there without caring if the owner of the company was his political rival. Anyway, my dear, who would ever have thought that a Rathis company would go bankrupt? Nobody. I still can't believe it. One of the most powerful families in the country, one of the most prestigious names. But that starving loser of a detective who lives from month to month can't possibly understand. That's when I realized it would do absolutely no good to talk to Pepe Pindonga, the guy has absolutely no power over the law, a poor sonofabitch who's being paid just so he can feed that crazy Diana some story or other. What I should have done is call that Deputy Chief Handal – even though I find him repulsive, even if he is a foul-mouthed busybody – so he can have a hand in this. I told Pepe Pindonga that I had to hang up. The worst part was that I couldn't find the famous little card where I'd written down the policeman's number. I had to turn my entire room upside down until I finally found it. What do you think happened? No matter how much I insisted, they kept telling me that the Deputy Chief was out on a special mission and they didn't know when he'd be back. At that very moment he must have been arresting Alberto, I was sure of it, you know my intuition never fails me, because I called Alberto again in order to give him a blast of what I'd discovered, but all his telephones were disconnected. I was just about to leave for Alberto's house to find out if they'd arrested him, tell Handal I absolutely had to talk to him, but just at that moment the phone rang. It was Pepe Pindonga again. He told me the police had just arrested Toñito Rathis, Alberto and all the other members of the board of directors of Finapro; this is just the beginning of what will undoubtedly end up being the swindle of the century. As you know, Pepe Pindonga worked at the police academy and he has excellent contacts there who pass him information. I asked him if that Deputy Chief Handal had taken part in the arrest. He told me he wasn't sure but most likely, because as chief of the Office of Investigations he had to be present. He suggested we meet tomorrow morning, early, to give him time to check out a few things, my theory about Alberto and Toñito Rathis being the masterminds behind Olga María's murder needs some solid proof, logic isn't enough, even less so now that they've arrested those guys for a multi-million-dollar financial fraud, people will think they're just being used as scapegoats to pin the blame on them for other crimes. That's what he told me. I answered him that he can investigate whatever he damn well wants to, the facts are there, clear as day, I don't need any proof: I've been turning it over in my head for more than a month, trying to figure out who could have ordered Olga María's murder. What does that Pepe Pindonga think, that other people are as stupid as he is? Do me a favour: I repeated that anybody who'd stolen millions of colones was capable of putting a contract out on somebody. I'm super-hyper, my dear; I feel electrified. I haven't stopped calling Deputy Chief Handal, but he still hasn't got back to his office. That's why I took a minute out to call you. I couldn't watch the telenovela any longer. There's nothing on the news yet; maybe there'll be something on the ten o'clock news. Who would have thought Alberto would end up like this? It's hard to imagine him part of a conspiracy, but after working so long with Toñito Rathis, something must have rubbed off on him. As soon as we hang up, I'm going to try again to get hold of this Deputy Chief Handal. I'm going to tell him exactly what he needs to do, tell him to stop wasting his time, like that Pepe Pindonga, such a sissy that detective turned out to be when I got worked up this afternoon, probably scares the daylights out of him to realize the mess he's stepped into. But it's Deputy Chief Handal's responsibility to investigate the case, to find the masterminds; he can't be satisfied with arresting the murderer, that horrible Robocop. That's why first thing he should find out about what kind of relationship Olga María and Alberto were having in the last few months. She wouldn't have told me anything. But it's easy to find out: you just have to ask the secretaries, the managers, to find out if Olga María visited or called either Alberto or Toñito Rathis frequently. That's the first step. When you've made a fixed-term investment you've got no reason to be visiting the bank all the time, only once when you invest and then again when the time is up. Right? That's the first thing Handal has to find out. I don't know, my dear. Look, the way things are going, nothing will surprise me now.

Olga María might have been involved in who knows what, and me like a drivelling idiot, totally clueless about all of it. Or they might have got her involved, without her even realizing it – considering Toñito Rathis's Machiavellian mind – in a plot that culminated in her death and Yuca's political demise. I swear I can't figure Olga María out at all. I thought I knew her, but now I realize she had many personalities. I still can't quite believe she had an *affaire* with Alberto. Here comes my mother, she looks very upset. Wait a second, she wants to tell me something. OK, she heard the news. She says everybody is going crazy. Yes, I know, Mama: they just arrested Alberto. Of course, and Toñito Rathis. Apparently it wasn't Yuca's money, according to my mama, it was Kati's and Don Federico's. Can you imagine? That's even worse for Alberto: getting into trouble with Don Federico Schultz is suicide. The Archbishop had a million colones in Finapro. Papa will be delighted to hear that: he'll say it's good for that priest to lose his money, serves him right for being so greedy, they should all go to hell. That's what Papa will say. I'll call you later, my dear – Mama isn't letting me talk, she's making a big fuss – and that way you can tell me what happened today in the telenovela. In a while I'll try again to get in touch with that Deputy Chief Handal. Ciao.

8. The Stampede

Robocop is following me! Open up! Hurry – I swear: it's him! Get inside, quick. Hopefully I shook him off. What a nightmare, my dear. Luckily I saw him in time. He was in a car parked in front of the house. Let me sit down. I can't catch my breath. Give me a glass of water. Horrendous, my dear. No, I'm not being paranoid. Look at how I'm shaking. What, you didn't hear he escaped yesterday afternoon? You probably haven't read the newspapers or seen the news. Pepe Pindonga just told me. Yes, my dear, I was on my way back from having breakfast with him and, just before I got to the house, I saw a car with tinted windows. It seemed weird that it was parked right smack in front of the house. I saw it just in time. It's one-two-three for emergencies, isn't it? What do you mean, how did I know it was him? It's not like I haven't seen his mug in the papers and on TV, not like I haven't dreamt about him, a criminal like that. Somebody else was in the driver's seat, and Robocop was sitting next to him. When I saw them I didn't slow down, I just ducked, like I was tuning the radio, and kept driving. Then, after turning the corner, I floored it and looked in the rear-view mirror to see if they were following me. I swear I didn't stop until I got here, I drove like a madwoman. Just a second, finally someone's answering. Hello, hello. I want to make a report, miss. That Robocop person, the one who murdered

Olga María de Trabanino, he was parked on Calle Las Magnolias ten minutes ago, in front of number twenty-five, in Colonia Utila, Santa Tecla. What do you mean, how do I know? I saw him. I'm Laura Rivera, Olga María's best friend. Robocop was parked in front of my house! What do you mean, what phone am I calling from? That's none of your business, you idiot. I'm telling you, a few minutes ago I saw that murderer parked in front of my house, waiting for me, stalking me. I damn well do have the right to insult you. It's because of you that that monster is going to get away. Instead of asking me stupid questions, call the nearest patrol cars so they can sweep the area. What's your name? I'm going to report you to Deputy Chief Handal, as an incompetent. If that criminal escapes, it's going to be your fault. I demand you tell me your name! You think I'm in the mood for your nonsense after finding that murderer in front of my house? That's more like it, finally, I get a reasonable response. It's a red car, I don't know, maybe a Toyota, pretty new, maybe this year's, with tinted glass. There are two: the other one in the driver's seat and Robocop. Don't you know he escaped from jail yesterday? So, hurry up, quick, alert the patrol cars. Do you hear me? Here, take the telephone, my dear. What an idiotic woman. She talked to me like I was the criminal. She said her name is Yésica Ramírez. I'm going to report her to Deputy Chief Handal. Yésica? Do me a favour! She's probably dark, short, with thick lips, and stupid, her name is Yésica. Let me look out the window: please God, don't let it be that Robocop has followed me.

What an idiot! I should have given her the address. I'm going to call her back. Give me the telephone. Hurry. I'm so distraught, I don't know what I'm doing. It's ringing again. I'm trembling. Why would he be following me? How did he know my address? He wants to kill me, my dear. I'm sure of it. Why was he waiting for me, then? They're answering. Yes, hello. I just called. I spoke to Yésica Ramírez, about Robocop, the murderer who escaped yesterday afternoon. I'd like to speak with her again. They're transferring me to her. Better to talk directly to her, so they don't get confused. Yes? Yésica? It's me again. Look, I'm going to give you the address where I am now, because if Robocop followed me he's probably in the vicinity. It's in Colonia Escalón, Seventh Street, between ninety-fifth and ninety-seventh avenue, number one-two-five-one. Did you alert the patrol cars? We'll keep our eyes peeled and, if we see Robocop's car drive by, we'll call you immediately. What are you waiting for? Hurry up, give this address to the police in the neighbourhood. Goodbye. People like that, my dear. Let's look out the window. Now what do we do? Oh no, the girls! God help us. Robocop probably wants to kill them. They're the only witnesses, the only ones who can identify him. We've got to call Marito. You dial. My hands are shaking. Here's his number at the advertising agency. That murderer is capable of going to their school to get them. Why didn't I think of that sooner?! It's busy? Try this other number. We've got to hurry and get the girls out of school. He's not there? How about his secretary? Let me talk to her. Look how my palms are sweating. Laura Rivera here. We urgently need to get in touch with Marito and tell him to take the girls out of school. The murderer who killed Olga María escaped yesterday afternoon. Didn't you see the papers? Give me his cell-phone number, and you call his beeper. Write it down, my dear: two-eight-six-one-eight-three-zero. What a nightmare! If he's already after me, he must be following everybody in Olga María's family, especially the girls. No answer. Marito, that brute, has his cell phone off. Hopefully, the secretary will find him. The thing is, I went to have breakfast with Pepe Pindonga, like I told you last night, so he could tell me what he found out about the relationship between Olga María and Alberto. We met at the Mister Donuts on El Paseo. He told me the news about Robocop's escape. Bring the newspaper over here. Let me see: it's inside. Because of that financial scandal with Finapro, nobody even realizes that criminal is on the loose. Listen: the guy escaped from his cell in the courthouse, yesterday afternoon, but the guards didn't realize it until night-time, when they checked on the prisoners. Can you believe it, somebody escapes from jail, he just wanders around as if he were puttering about his own house, then pretends to be a prisoner they're releasing? Smells fishy to me. It's a conspiracy, my dear. And on the same day they uncover Finapro's multi-million-dollar fraud? That's what I told Pepe Pindonga a while ago, while we were having breakfast: it seems obvious that Robocop's escape was planned to coincide with Toñito Rathis and Alberto's arrest. Let's call Marito's office again to find out if the secretary got hold of him. Afterwards, I'll call Deputy Chief Handal. Can you believe it, I couldn't get hold of him last night? He's buried up to his eyeballs in the Finapro case, that's why he hasn't returned my calls. He's probably already let the trail get cold that leads to the masterminds who planned Olga María's murder, but Robocop's escape will force him to pay more attention to the case. That's what I told Pepe Pindonga, too. The telephone in Marito's office is always busy. I'd do anything to save those girls, but what if Robocop is here? Look, look, there's the patrol car. We're in luck. If we don't find Marito, I'll ask the police to escort me to the American School, and we can bring the girls here. We've also got to talk to Julita and Doña Olga and Sergio. That fiend could attack any one of them. Finally, the call went through. Hello, Laura Rivera here. Did you find Marito? I can't believe it. Nobody knows where he is? Keep trying – it's extremely urgent. Look for him everywhere. OK, bye. Incredible, my dear – Marito simply left half an hour ago, without telling anybody where he was going, and he left his beeper on his desk. It makes me furious, he's so stupid. I bet he's in some motel with one of those waitresses he's got the hots for – the depraved pervert – while Robocop is out here threatening us all. I'll lay you odds. I'm going to call Doña Olga. The patrol car drove by again, didn't it? The line's busy. Maybe we can find Sergio or Cuca, and get one of them to go pick up the girls. Well, Pepe Pindonga told me it's too soon to find out anything about the relationship between Olga María and Alberto during the last few months. The police have put all the financial company employees in virtual quarantine. Nobody's answering at Sergio's, how weird, the housekeeper isn't even there. I'm going to try Julita. You know what Pepe Pindonga told me? That the only way to find out if Toñito Rathis and Alberto are behind Olga María's murder is to talk to Yuca: he must know something that would help us get to the bottom of this. That's what he said. Then I told him that the money he had in Finapro wasn't his, Yuca's, it was Don Federico's and Kati's. Pepe Pindonga just whistled. Here she is. Julita. It's Laura, I'm so glad I got hold of you. Have you heard? Robocop escaped. I saw him in front of my house, my dear Julita. I'm terrified. Very worried about the girls. That fiend wouldn't think twice about killing them. May he burn in hell. But I can't find Marito! He's not in his office, his cell phone is off, and he left his beeper on his desk. Do you have any idea where he might be? You don't know. It's urgent that somebody go and pick up the girls and take them to a safe place. And you, you be careful, Julita. That murderer is going to return to the scene of the crime. You must be careful. Don't open the door to anybody. Try not to go out. They say murderers always return to the scene of the crime. And the girls? God help us! They'll have to stay at Doña Olga's house or at Sergio's or they can bring them to me if Marito wants, but no way in the world should they return to the house until they capture that fiend. Do you know how Doña Olga is doing? I hope she doesn't have a heart attack. All calamities occur at once. I've tried to call her but the line is busy. Sergio and

Cuca must be there. Take care of yourself, Julita. I'm going to call the police right now so they'll send a patrol car to protect them, because I'm certain that any moment now Robocop is going to show up in front of the house. It's a red car, with tinted glass. Be careful. If you talk to Marito, warn him. OK, bye. Poor Julita, I'm going to try Deputy Chief Handal once more – I dialled his number so many times last night I've learnt it by heart. The patrol car hasn't driven by? You should go outside and check if there are any suspicious cars parked along the block. Hello. Yes? It's urgent, I must speak with Deputy Chief Handal. Look, miss, this is Laura Rivera. I've been trying to call him since last night and I haven't been able to reach him. But now it's extremely urgent. Tell him I just saw Robocop in front of my house. He's the one who murdered Olga María de Trabanino, the one who escaped from jail yesterday. Yes, the very one. I already called one-two-three. But it's urgent I speak to the Deputy Chief. Tell him I have something extremely important to tell him about the case. He's got to send agents to protect Olga María's family, because that murderer is planning to kill them. Get in touch with him right now, through your internal system. Tell him to call me at my number in Colonia Escalón. I'll give it to you just to make sure: two-six-four-seven-nine-eight-two. And hurry! Goodbye. Why don't you go take a look, my dear, while I try to call Doña Olga again? Don't be afraid. The patrol cars should be nearby. That murderer doesn't know you. Finally, the call's going through. What luck. Hello. Cuca? It's Laura, my dear. How's Doña Olga?

Oh, no, I was afraid of that. OK, so don't tell her about Robocop. You know, don't you? I'm so glad she's not allowed to watch television or look at the newspapers. I'm very worried. We should get the girls out of school right now. That criminal is on the loose and I'm afraid he's going to hurt them. Don't you agree? I saw him in front of my house in Santa Tecla. Yes, my dear, it was him. He was parked right smack in front of my door. Luckily, I saw him and kept driving. I don't know if he followed me. I'm in Escalón now, but I'm afraid to go outside. That's why I've been calling Marito to tell him to go pick up the girls. But nobody knows where he is. Could Sergio go? Call him at work. It's a matter of life and death. I have a premonition that he's going to attack them. Remember, they're the principal witnesses. I don't know, my dear, why he would come after me. The only thing I know for sure is that it was him. I already called the police. The police are patrolling the area. Even so, I'm still afraid to go out. You've got to stay there and take care of Doña Olga. Send her my regards. Don't let her hear anything. It would be terrible for her if she found out that that criminal is on the loose. Call me after you talk to Sergio. So I can feel reassured. I want to ask Deputy Chief Handal to send somebody to guard the American School. We'll be in touch. Ciao. You didn't feel like going out? I don't blame you. Let's wait a bit. I'm going to leave the telephone alone in case Handal is trying to call me. What a nightmare. Everything has happened at once: the loss of Olga María's money, Alberto's arrest, Doña Olga's illness, Robocop's escape – I feel like I'm in a movie. Then that murderer gets it into his head to come after me. I need some lime-blossom tea, to calm my nerves. Will you make it for me? I'm going to call Papa. I don't know what else to do. Yes, he's still at the finca; he'll be back this afternoon. Mama is at the beauty salon. The only thing she'd do is get worried and make things worse. Hello, Filo, may I speak to my father? Thanks. Oh, Papito, you have no idea what's happening to me! That criminal, Robocop, the one who killed Olga María, yesterday he escaped from jail and I saw him a while ago parked in front of my house. I'm terrified. I came up here, to Escalón. I already called the police and they're patrolling the area. But I don't understand why he'd come after me. It's horrible, Papito. I'm going to stay here; yes, don't worry. What I'm most worried about is that he'll go after Olga María's daughters. Because they're the only witnesses. You won't be here till the afternoon? As soon as I get hold of Deputy Chief Handal, I'm going to ask him to come here and personally escort me to my house. I haven't been able to get in touch with him: it's because he's also in charge of the Finapro case. But I'm hoping he'll call me now, because Robocop's escape is a huge setback for him. Don't worry, Papito, I won't go out alone. Big kisses. Ciao. Did the water boil, my dear? Make me a very strong cup of tea, with two bags, I need a double dose. Why doesn't anybody answer, neither Deputy Chief Handal or Marito? I'm so anxious. Nothing like this has ever happened to me. Just look at what Olga María's death has unleashed. I can't believe it. I'm going to put a lot of sugar in it: they say sugar helps counteract the adrenaline. I read it in *Vanidades*. Let's look out the window. What I want is for a patrol car to park right here in front so that murderer won't have the slightest doubt that, if he gets anywhere near this house, they'll nab him. That's the only way I'll feel safe. But the police must be around somewhere. You're right – what an idiot I am. They don't want to tip him off. Finally! I'll answer it. Hello. Deputy Chief? I've been trying to get hold of you all day. I urgently need to speak to you in person. I sure did see him. What? You don't believe me? It was Robocop, in front of my house in Santa Tecla. But I also want to talk to you about some other things: the relationship between the collapse of Finapro and Olga María's murder. I'd rather talk to you in person. Are you coming here? In how long? I'm not planning on going anywhere with that psychopath chasing me. Come as soon as you can. In half an hour. I won't budge; not on my life. But make sure your agents are as nearby as possible, because if that murderer shows up I don't want him to have time even to ring the doorbell. The most important thing, Deputy Chief: you have to send policemen to protect the girls, Olga María's daughters. Robocop is going to try to hurt them. I'm positive. They must have around-the-clock protection. It's your responsibility. I hope so. Goodbye. That imbecile doesn't believe I actually saw Robocop: I could hear it in his tone of voice. I held my tongue because I need him to come – I didn't want to give him any excuse to leave me in the lurch, but he isn't completely convinced that Robocop was waiting for me in front of my house. You're going to have to change the upholstery on this armchair; it's very worn out. Where did Marito go? Call the agency again. No, wait a minute. I'm going to call Pepe Pindonga, maybe he's already arrived at his office. What are you seeing, my dear? Oh no, oh my God! That's the car! Definitely! It's Robocop's car! Did you see it? It's here! Call one-two-three! It didn't stop? But that was him. It's busy. What are we going to do? You say there was only a driver? I didn't notice. I only saw it from behind. But it was going very slowly, as if they're looking for the house. I left my car right in front – how stupid of me! I should have put it in the garage. I'm sure he already recognized it. He followed me, my dear! I knew it. Call one-two-three again or call Handal. Oh, my God. Move over, we don't want him to see you at the window if he drives by again. Are you sure there was only the driver in the car? That's even worse, my dear. That means Robocop already got out and is sneaking around nearby. Don't open the door for anything in the world. Let's double-lock it. Did they answer? Give me the phone. Quick, it's an emergency, I must speak with Yésica Ramírez! Hurry, the murderer is here, outside the house! Call the patrols! Robocop's red car just drove by the house! No, it didn't stop. It was only the driver. That means Robocop is hiding right here, in the doorway, waiting for someone to leave. No, I haven't seen him but I know he's there. They have to get here immediately! Do you hear me? Idiot. She asks if I actually saw him. She wants me to go out to the street so that murderer can shoot me. Oh, my God, such terror. Let's pray. I know that man is outside. I can sense it. Why don't the police cars show up? That stupid woman hasn't called them. They should be here already. And Deputy Chief Handal? Why is he taking so long? They didn't want to give me his cell-phone number. The secretary says he doesn't have one, they communicate over their walkie-talkies. But that's a lie: when have you ever seen a chief of police without a cell phone? I'm going to have some more tea. Listen! Listen! A car just parked in front of the house. Peek out the window. Shit, I tripped on that fucking table. Damn! I banged myself really hard, right on the knee. Is that the police? Let me see. Move over. Oh, my God! It can't be! It's Robocop's car! Where are the police? What are they waiting for? They're both coming, the same two who were waiting for me in front of my house in Santa Tecla: Robocop and the driver! Look at them, they're getting out of the car. They're coming this way! What should we do? My God! It's not the driver: it's a woman! His accomplice, my dear. Hand me the telephone. Let's go into the back, in case they start shooting at the door and the windows. Run! One-two-three is busy. Why don't the police arrest them? I don't hear any cars or sirens. They're ringing the doorbell! We're lost! Let me dial Deputy Chief Handal's number. Don't even think of opening the door! Those criminals keep ringing the bell. What are we going to do? Handal's number is busy, too! They're going to kill us, my dear! We have nowhere to run! They keep ringing the bell! They know we're here! Why doesn't Deputy Chief Handal get here already? They're trying to break down the door! Look: it's that woman with the short hair, that's Robocop's accomplice, the one who looks like a man! What are you saying? Did you hear? They're shouting my name! What's wrong with them?! Do they think I'm going to open, that they're going to trick me?! Those criminals are crazy! Let me call one-two-three again! Hello! Hello! This is an emergency: put Yésica Ramírez on the line! Hurry! Yésica! Call the police immediately: Robocop is here, he's trying to break down the door! I don't understand why the police aren't coming to arrest him! He's with a woman! Listen to how they're banging down the door! They want to kill me! Help! How am I supposed to calm down when those murderers are right outside my door?! Any minute now they're going to break in! I'm not going to hang up until I hear the sirens! The sirens are the only thing that will scare them away! Call Deputy Chief Handal! He told me he was on his way here! What's wrong with that idiot, why isn't he here?! Don't hang up! Call him on another line! I'm ordering you: don't hang up! It's the only way I can feel a little safer: if they come in here and kill me at least you'll hear it! They keep banging on the door! They're about to break it down! The woman is calling out my name! Oh, my God! The sirens! They're getting closer! Thank you, Yésica, you've saved my life. Goodbye! The sirens are out in front. They've stopped banging on the door. Probably the criminals are trying to escape. Let's be careful, my dear. Any minute the shooting will start. They turned off the sirens. Maybe they already nabbed them. I can hear voices outside. Let's peek out the window. Hopefully they're taking them away. Look, I don't believe it: the policemen are talking to the criminals! Why don't they round them up, put them in handcuffs, and get them into the patrol cars once and for all?! Look at them: they're coming this way, acting like old friends! I don't understand, my dear. Something's fishy here. Something very strange is going on. They're ringing the doorbell again. We're not going to open it. They must be co-conspirators. That's why that criminal escaped, because the police are in cahoots with him! That's the only explanation! Let's just keep quiet! I know what they want: when we open the door, feeling safe because the police are here, Robocop will gun us down and then they'll let him escape. That's the plan for getting rid of us, so we don't tell anybody what we've discovered! I bet Robocop and the police work for Toñito Rathis and Alberto! Another siren, my dear! This'll ruin their plan! They've stopped ringing the doorbell. Let's look out the window again. Don't show yourself. It's Deputy Chief Handal! What a relief, we're saved! But what's going on?! He's talking to the criminals, too, like they're old friends! Now we're really lost! They're going to kill us! Handal is the one behind the whole operation! I should have guessed! Filthy! Corrupt! Oh, what terror! They're taking advantage of us being here alone. Help, Papa! They're ringing again! It's Handal's voice! What are we going to do?! They're going to break down the door! I can't stand it any more, my dear! There's no escape! That Arab Handal is a traitor! We can't let them kill us in here! Our only hope is to get out into the street, so the neighbours will see, so they'll know we've been captured alive! I'm going to open the door and run out, screaming! Are you ready?! Now! Traitor! Handal! Help! Don't kill us! Murderers!

9. The Clinic

Good thing they let you in, my dear. They've had me incommunicado. Only my parents have been allowed to visit me. The truth is I've been sleeping most of my time here. It's been almost three days and it feels like nothing. The one who visits the most is Dr Romo; he's so understanding. He says I'll get better soon, I had a nervous breakdown because of all the stress of Olga María's murder and Robocop's escape. Good thing you managed to escape, otherwise they would have shut you up in here, too. I don't remember anything after we made that dash for it and those policemen attacked us. The wretches. They sedated me: I spent a whole day sleeping, that's what Dr Romo explained to me. Papa's very worried. He says I'll need to leave the country to be able to relax and recuperate, I need to be in a different atmosphere, forget all these calamities. The worst part is that the minute I woke up I started worrying about the girls and what Robocop might do to them. Can you imagine how I felt: waking up after sleeping a whole day on sedatives, in a strange bed, in an unknown room? I thought they'd kidnapped me, I thought Robocop and Deputy Chief Handal saw it was impossible to liquidate me in front of the neighbours so they brought me here. And it was precisely at that moment that the nurse came in: I was standing up, rummaging through the drawers, checking the medicines on the bedside table, peeking out through the blinds, figuring out how to escape. I was scared to death when I heard the door opening; I thought it was them. The nurse was surprised, too, seeing me standing up. She told me to go back to bed, I still needed to recuperate, I needed absolute rest. That was yesterday, about mid-morning. I flooded her with questions: where was I, who'd brought me here, who'd visited me, when could I leave this place. The poor thing didn't know what to say, but right then Mama appeared behind her. She hugged me, she was crying, as if I'd risen from the dead; she asked me to lie down again and told the nurse to call Dr Romo to come and check on me. I felt horrible, my dear. I warned her that there was no way I was going to allow the doctor to see me looking like that. I went into the bathroom to wash my face and brush my hair, make myself look vaguely presentable. The doctor is so elegant, so distinguished-looking, and I wasn't going to receive him as if he were a servant or something. God help me. I already told you a ton about him: I've been going to him for three years once a month. Good thing Mama brought a few of my things, and I could fix myself up a bit, though this hair, my dear, if I don't go to Mercedes's salon, it looks horrendous. But you know what happened? Dr Romo couldn't come right away, so I had to listen to my mother's version. She says I suffered an acute attack of paranoia, that's why I confused Robocop with a couple of journalists waiting for me in front of my house. I don't believe her. Mama swallows anything they tell her. She told me not to worry about the girls: the police are certain that Robocop has left the country, they think he went to Honduras, so we're not in any danger. That's what Handal and his henchmen told her. That's when I asked her who brought me to this clinic and how it happened. According to her, when we dashed out of the house, my nerves gave out and I passed out right in front the police. Did you see that? As far as I'm concerned, those swine took advantage of the uproar to beat me up or inject me with some narcotic. Because I don't remember anything, as you know. The thing is, when I fainted, Handal called the house and Mama told him to bring me to Dr Romo's clinic. But I didn't keep talking to Mama about it, especially after she came to me with her song and dance about how if I went to church more often, if I led a more devout life, I wouldn't have so many problems with my nerves. When she talks like that, I can't stand it. That's why I changed the subject. I asked her about the Brazilian telenovela. It made me so mad to be missing the last few episodes. The doctor has forbidden me from watching television for a week: he says the news could upset me. He hasn't relented, even though I've sworn I won't watch anything other than the telenovela. Good thing Mama has been telling me what's going on: I just hope that Holofernes – he's so gorgeous – doesn't get killed. That's what Mama was doing, summing up the episodes of the telenovela I'd missed, when Dr Romo came in. That man is so elegant, my dear, he's so debonair, so tall and handsome. Right off the bat I told him how horrible I felt, how I'd never want him to see me like this, without my hair done or make-up on, as is only proper. He told me I looked beautiful, even my tired face was a delight to look at. A man like that is very disarming, my dear. I'd only ever seen him in his office, where we've only just talked. But yesterday, after he asked Mama to leave us alone for a moment, when he started examining me, and I felt his hands on my body, I swear I got extremely turned on. It was overwhelming, my dear, I got wet when he touched me to check my blood pressure, my pulse and all the rest. I felt like pulling him into bed with me right then and there. I don't know, maybe from too much sleep, or because of the drugs, but the truth is I felt a lot going on down there between my legs. I was melting. And that man was aware of everything that was going on, because he immediately took his hands off me, he said I was doing much better but I needed a week of absolute rest to effect a complete recovery. There was one moment, I swear, when I was on the verge of grabbing his crotch and starting to rub him; I had this uncontrollable urge to put it in my mouth. That's why he moved away, in his best professional manner. He said this breakdown was very serious, I shouldn't take it lightly, and once I get stronger we'll talk more. I wanted to hold on to him, ask him about the medications, about the relationship between what he called my schizophrenic tendencies and the attack of paranoia. The only thing he said was that the stress was to blame; I haven't been able to get over the death of my best friend, and then that murderer's escape provoked the crisis. That's how he explained it. Then he said he had to go, he'd check in on me later in the afternoon. Since then he's always come in with a nurse, as if she were his bodyguard. I've been tempted to tell him that I need to talk to him alone, but I haven't had another episode like that first one, when I felt so aroused. At least when I'm awake, because that same afternoon I had the strangest dream about Dr Romo: we were in a restroom at the airport, I don't know which one, and I pulled down his trousers and his underwear, and the doctor just let me do whatever I wanted, I rubbed his balls between the palms of my hands, and just as I was kneeling down to take him in my mouth, Olga María appeared behind him and started scolding me for such behaviour in a public place, and then I was surrounded by Pepe Pindonga, Deputy Chief Handal, Yuca, Alberto, and they were all threatening me, demanding I be arrested for crimes against public morality and decency, and when I turned to Dr Romo for help, he'd disappeared. That's when I woke up, terrified. Quite a dream to have in the afternoon, maybe that's why I haven't got so turned on by Dr Romo again in quite the same way. But I was telling you about the morning. When the doctor left, Mama came in again and warned me that Deputy Chief Handal has made it his business to get into my room. According to her, as soon as he finds out I've woken up, that detective will try to get in and question me. But the clinic has strict orders not to allow this. Only with a subpoena, Papa said. No way I'd want to see that fool's ugly face. If he finds out everything I've discovered about the relationships between Olga María, Alberto and

Toñito Rathis, who knows what he'd be capable of. Even worse after what Pepe Pindonga told me. What, I didn't tell you yet? Well, yesterday afternoon, after that weirdest of dreams about the doctor, when I opened my eyes, who do you think was sitting in that very chair, acting like Mr Nice Guy? I thought I was still dreaming, until the famous detective said hello and asked how I was feeling. At first I got cross, what nerve, sneaking into my room without authorization. I told him to leave immediately, I said he was being disrespectful, I'm sick and the doctor has strictly forbidden me from talking to imbeciles. I gave it to him straight, I left no room for any doubts. I warned him that if he didn't get out immediately, I'd start to scream. He begged me to calm down, he said that if he'd made such an effort to get in here it was so he could tell me something that might interest me. That made me curious, because it was obvious this Pepe Pindonga had found out something new about Olga María's case. I asked him how he'd managed to get into my room. He told me he bribed a nurse, but he didn't want to reveal her name. I'm sure he used some other trick. Did you know my father put one of his own personal security guards on duty at the door of this room? How could that Pepe Pindonga have got in, eh? I learnt from him that the journalists in front of my house were Rita Mena, the reporter, and that photographer nicknamed Zompopo. Pepe says I got Zompopo and Robocop confused: they've got the same kind of square head and, sitting in the car, without seeing their bodies, it was easy to make that mistake. I finally believed him at noon today when the nurse told me that a lady journalist from *Ocho Columnas* has tried to get in to see me but was told I'm not allowed any visitors. Pepe explained that that busybody wants to interview me in connection with Olga María's case: she's writing an article about Robocop and, now that the killer has escaped, she's in a rush to finish it. Filthy rat, how could she imagine I would talk to her after what she did to Yuca? By the way, Pepe talked to Yuca and mentioned to him my idea about Alberto and Toñito Rathis being behind Olga María's murder. He was in shock. Here's what Pepe told me: Yuca opened his eyes very wide and asked him where I'd got such an idea. Seems I hit the nail on the head, my dear, by the looks of it. Yuca didn't know about the *affaire* between Olga María and Alberto, and he didn't tell Pepe Pindonga anything, but, based on his reaction, I know I got it right. I bet Yuca tries to call me any minute now, but they aren't letting any calls through either, doctor's orders. I hope Yuca decides to come. I've given him all the clues he needs to find out who's plotting against him. Now, with the scandal of Finapro's crash, it'll all be as clear as day to him. Like it is to me. The only one who refuses to understand is that Deputy Chief Handal. Why would he want to, though, since he's part of the conspiracy? He's probably been receiving money from Toñito Rathis: that's why he let Robocop escape, that's why he wanted to be there for Toñito's arrest, to make sure he was treated well. You know what he's come up with now, according to what Pepe Pindonga told me? He's started investigating some of Robocop's commanding officers in the Acahuapa battalion during the war. Only somebody interested in confusing the issue would think up such nonsense. It turns out that one of them, some major or other, went into business once the war was over, offering security services to important businessmen and landowners, one of them being Papa. Can you believe what that cop wastes his time doing? And since he doesn't dare question Papa, because that's getting in way over his head, he wants to talk to me to find out if I know anything about this Major What's-His-Face, who might have hired Robocop to murder Olga María. What an idiot. I don't remember that major very well, I might have seen him a couple of times when I visited Papa, if it's the same man; he might even be somebody I introduced to Olga María – pure coincidence – because she happened to come by the house while he was waiting in the living room. I wouldn't be surprised if Handal tried to throw suspicion on me so I'd be forced to keep quiet about what I know. Easy, my dear: he could say that Robocop was hired by Major What's-His-Face, on my orders, because I was fighting with Olga María for Yuca. Those bastards are capable of saying that I hired somebody to kill my best friend because of a man, as if Yuca would be worth it. I swear: they're capable of saying anything: I was jealous of her, I'm under psychiatric treatment, she was like my alter ego I had to get rid of, Yuca has always been the man of my life, and he never paid any attention to me because of Olga María, I still resented her for destroying my marriage with Alberto, I hated her because she always put me down, any old nonsense. I get furious just thinking about all the money they waste paying that gang of corrupt policemen. Just wait, you'll see how they'll do absolutely everything they can to divert the investigation of Olga María's murder away from the paths that lead to Alberto and Toñito Rathis's fraudulent schemes. Because Pepe Pindonga told me another rumour that fills in all the gaps: it turns out that Finapro's money was used to pay a debt Toñito and his group had with the Cali Cartel; that's what they're saying in the inner circles of the police and the newspapers: they didn't steal the depositors' money for the electoral campaign, or for the soccer team's travel expenses, or to cover up holes in the other Rathis companies, but to pay off debts between drug traffickers. Do you remember that scandal about a multi-million-dollar shipment of cocaine they found in a container in the Port of Acajutla, in the warehouse of a shipping company Toñito Rathis owns stock in? There's the key, my dear. Who knows what Olga María might have found out, and that's why they killed her, for being nosey, for sleeping with people she shouldn't have slept with. That's exactly what I told Pepe Pindonga, before telling him to leave, because I felt tired, or rather disheartened, depressed. It's awful, my dear, with Olga María's murder the same thing will happen that happens with all the crimes committed in this country: the authorities will never find out anything and people will simply forget about it. That's what I was thinking about after Pepe Pindonga left. It's awful what I'm feeling:

something between sadness and anger. I want to do something so that everybody will know that Toñito Rathis and Alberto have something to do with our friend's death. But in here, I'm screwed. That's why I don't know if I'm going to tolerate being cooped up in here for very long. I'd like to get out, I want to really stir things up. Though maybe nobody would give me any support, not even Yuca: as you know, politicians have their own interests. Papa won't let me, either. I'm so sick of Mama: she says my nerves are a mess, there's something wrong with my head, since Olga María died I've changed, I spend all my time talking to myself, I always go out alone, as if she didn't know I was with you. She says she's very worried. The same old story. The only thing I can do is leave the country, like they're recommending, take a long vacation, especially if that Deputy Chief Handal tries to harass me with his Major What's-His-Face. I'll leave and go to Miami, to Diana. Maybe she'll give me some support and from there we can do something, but without that trash, Pepe Pindonga. Anything is possible. What worries me is what will happen to you in my absence – who will you talk to, who will you go out with, how will you keep from getting bored? If only Olga María were still...